Welcome to the Secret World of Alex Mack!

I thought going to a Renaissance fair with my friends would be a cool way to learn about the Middle Ages. But when a stray leather ball hit me in the head, I completely lost my memory! I didn't know who I was, but it didn't take me long to realize I had some pretty amazing powers. Let me explain. . . .

I'm Alex Mack. I was just another average kid until my first day of junior high.

One minute I'm walking home from school—the next there's a *crash!* A truck from the Paradise Valley Chemical plant overturns in front of me, and I'm drenched in some weird chemical.

And since then—well, nothing's been the same. I can move objects with my mind, shoot electrical charges through my fingertips, and morph into a liquid shape . . . which is handy when I get in a tight spot!

My best friend, Ray, thinks it's cool—and my sister, Annie, thinks I'm a science project.

They're the only two people who know about my new powers. I can't let anyone else find out—not even my parents—because I know the chemical plant wants to find me and turn me into some experiment.

But you know something? I guess I'm not so average anymore!

The Secret World of Alex Mack™

Alex, You're Glowing!
Bet You Can't!
Bad News Babysitting!
Witch Hunt!
Mistaken Identity!
Cleanup Catastrophe!
Take a Hike!
Go for the Gold!
Poison in Paradise!
Zappy Holidays! (Super Edition)
Junkyard Jitters!
Frozen Stiff!
I Spy!
High Flyer!
Milady Alex!

Available from MINSTREL Books

NICKELODEON®

the secret world of

ALEX MACK™

Milady Alex!

Diana G. Gallagher

A MINSTREL® BOOK

Published by POCKET BOOKS
New York   London   Toronto   Sydney   Tokyo   Singapore

This book is a work of fiction. Names, characters, places and inci-
dents are products of the author's imagination or are used ficti-
tiously. Any resemblance to actual events or locales or persons,
living or dead, is entirely coincidental.

A MINSTREL PAPERBACK *Original*

 A Minstrel Book published by
POCKET BOOKS, a division of Simon & Schuster Inc.
1230 Avenue of the Americas, New York, NY 10020

Copyright © 1997 by Viacom International Inc., and RHI Entertain-
ment, Inc. All rights reserved. Based on the Nickelodeon series enti-
tled "The Secret World of Alex Mack."

All rights reserved, including the right to reproduce
this book or portions thereof in any form whatsoever.
For information address Pocket Books, 1230 Avenue
of the Americas, New York, NY 10020

ISBN: 0-671-00684-3

First Minstrel Books printing May 1997

10 9 8 7 6 5 4 3 2

NICKELODEON and all related titles, logos and characters
are trademarks of Viacom International, Inc.

A MINSTREL BOOK and colophon are registered trademarks of
Simon & Schuster Inc.

Front cover photo by Pat Hill Studio

Printed in the U.S.A.

For Dane Isbell,
who understands the value of honor
and is a true friend of mine

Milady Alex!

me I gotta lose the watch, too." Muttering, Louis stuffed the watch in his pocket. "Whose bright idea was this anyway?"

Everyone looked at Alex.

"When I suggested it, you all thought hanging out at a fair was better than spending days doing research at the library and the museum," Alex reminded them.

"I still do." Ray grinned. "Giving a ten-minute speech on how we spent a day living in the past sure beats writing a twenty-page term paper on it."

"Good point." Louis sighed. "I guess this getup isn't that bad."

"Louis." Robyn eyed him pointedly. "You're wearing regular clothes. What's the big deal?"

Alex nodded. The fun would be spoiled if everyone didn't get into the spirit of the festival. Wearing medieval clothes was part of the hands-on history project. Louis and Ray were both decked out in black jeans, short boots, white shirts, and vests. Even though their outfits were ordinary, they still blended in. Robyn had on a long, flower-print skirt and a peasant blouse with sandals. Nicole had borrowed her mother's long, forest-green skirt with matching vest. A long-sleeved white blouse and buckled ankle boots completed her outfit.

Wanting to look as authentic as possible, Alex had done some research on women's fashions during the time of King Richard the Lion-Hearted. She had bought several yards of a coarse, off-white fabric to make the basic T-dress. She had simply folded it over and cut out the neckline. Then she had cut the folded material to look like a T and stitched up the wide arm and side seams. Cinched with a wide belt, the dress looked remarkably like the picture in the book. Her lace-up ankle boots matched the brown leather belt she had found at the thrift store.

The only modern device the group carried with them besides money and Louis's watch was Robyn's camera. Pictures would almost guarantee them an A for their report.

"It could be worse," Ray observed as a young man walked by wearing a lace-up green tunic over a shirt with billowing sleeves, and knee-high boots over tight brown pants. The man's Robin Hood hat sported a long feather.

"So quit complaining, Louis." Nicole leveled a serious scowl at him, then grinned. "You might even have fun."

"And learn something, too," Alex said as she started toward the gate into the festival grounds.

"I wouldn't count on that too much, Alex," Robyn said. "The SCA runs these events in a way that idealizes back then—not like things actually were."

"The SC—what?" Ray gave his money to a gate guard wearing the pleated plaid kilt of a Scottish highland clan.

"The Society for Creative Anachronism." Robyn put her change in a small, drawstring cloth purse looped through her belt. "This whole Renaissance Festival is an anachronism because it's several hundred years out of date."

"I feel as if I just stepped out of a time machine." Ray peered down the dirt track that cut through the woods. A woman with a flowered wreath in her braided hair walked beside a knight dressed in chain mail and a cloth coat of arms from the Crusades. He led a horse through a crowd of early-morning sightseers wearing normal summer clothes.

Alex felt a rush of excitement as they joined the people on the road. Brightly colored pennants and banners were visible through the trees and the lilting strains of a medieval melody rose above the buzz of the crowd. History was one of her favorite subjects in school, but Alex was particularly fascinated by the long-ago days of noble knights and elegant ladies, castles and kings.

"Something sure smells good." Louis's face brightened as he sniffed the tantalizing aroma of freshly baked bread.

"Another anachronism." Robyn nodded emphatically. "Back in the real Middle Ages everything was dirty and stank. And the peasants were not happy-go-lucky farmers living a simple carefree life, either."

"She's right about that," Alex said sadly. "The kings gave land to the nobles and knights who helped them fight their wars. The serfs farmed it, but they didn't own anything, not even their crops."

"And the peasants couldn't leave the land they worked." Nicole threw up her hands in disgust. "They couldn't even marry without the landholder's permission. There weren't any civil rights for the poor under the feudal system."

"Hold it." Louis stopped and held up his hands. "So if this fair isn't how it really was, why are we here?"

"The crafts and games and some of the food and the music are all reproduced authentically," Alex said patiently.

"And the SCA uses the same basic code of honor and rules the knights and nobles followed," Robyn added.

"So even though the people pretending to be peasants here are happy and well fed," Nicole said, "it's still sort of the way it was back in the year twelve hundred."

Ray clamped a hand on Louis's shoulder. "And we'll have a good time, too."

"I doubt it, Ray. This is totally uncool."

"Suit yourself, Louis." Alex adjusted her belt. "You can always write a twenty-page museum report instead."

"Forget that!" Ray inhaled deeply. "I'm going to get some of that bread."

"I'm with you." Louis shrugged in surrender. "That smell is hard to resist."

"I don't think I'm ready for food just yet." Robyn wrinkled her nose.

"We don't have to stay together all the time," Nicole said. "Let's just meet every hour or so to compare notes."

"Where?" Alex asked.

"Right there." Ray pointed to a large tree in the center of a small clearing. Stone benches circled the trunk under the shade of the leafy branches.

Alex stared as they paused on the edge of the clearing. Rustic wooden booths and colored tents with pointed tops ringed the perimeter of the open space. Paths lined with more booths meandered through the surrounding woods. A raised, tented platform with two thrones sat on the edge of a large, roped-off field directly ahead. Banners decorated with coats of arms fluttered atop tall poles that ringed the arena where the jousts and other make-believe combat competitions would take place. Dozens of people bustled about more tents on the far side of the field.

"Okay. If anybody wants to connect, wait at the tree." Robyn's eyes widened as she stared past Ray's shoulder. "That's an elephant!"

"Right," Louis scoffed. "There weren't any elephants in medieval Europe, were there?"

Nicole shrugged.

"Don't know, but I gotta get a picture." Robyn waved and started across the clearing with Nicole.

Alex curtsied demurely in front of the boys. "Catch ya later, m'lords."

Ray bowed in return. "At your service, milady."

"Oh, give me a break!" Grabbing Ray's arm, Louis hauled him off to find the bread booth.

Laughing, Alex ran to catch up with Robyn and

Nicole. At least Ray seemed willing to lose himself in a Middle Ages fantasy for a day. She was sure even Louis would get with the program before long. *It would be almost impossible not to,* Alex thought as she absorbed the sights, sounds, and smells of the fair.

A man sat on a tree stump playing a lute and singing. Alex recognized the tune. She had heard it in a dozen different TV commercials. She just hadn't realized the song was centuries old and had words. A juggler dressed as a court jester with bells on his hat and pointed shoes dazzled half a dozen small children as he kept five balls moving from one hand to the other.

The aroma of roasted turkey legs and buttered corn on the cob hung in the air, drawing crowds to the food stands in spite of the early hour. Elaborate, embroidered dresses and surcoats hung from ropes strung between trees. Another booth sold wooden shields emblazoned with various coats of arms. The heraldic designs that had once been worn to identify members of a particular family were popular with people who still bore the old and honored names.

Almost half the people were in costumes. Although, Alex realized, their clothing represented historic periods ranging anywhere between the years 600 and 1600. After they had done some basic research, Alex and her friends had chosen twelve hundred as a happy medium. Besides, they were all familiar with the Robin Hood legend during the late eleven hundreds when King Richard had left England to lead the Third Crusade in the Middle East.

Robyn gasped as they stopped by the fenced elephant ride area. "It's so big!"

Huge, Alex thought. The woman leading the elephant around the enclosure was dwarfed by the largest land animal on earth. A box draped with red and yellow cloth was attached to the elephant's back like a saddle. Four people sat inside it.

"One of us should be in the picture," Robyn said as she checked the camera's settings. "Who's gonna volunteer?"

"I'd rather not—on principle," Nicole explained. "I don't believe in the exploitation of animals."

"Don't look at me!" Robyn's freckled face paled. "I'm taking the picture. Besides, heights make me dizzy."

Nicole turned to Alex. "You always wanted to ride an elephant, right, Alex?"

"You're kidding." Alex glanced at the unbelievably big elephant. The handler stopped it by a tall wooden platform from which people climbed in and out of the box-saddle. Then she looked back at Robyn and Nicole's expectant faces.

"We'll all chip in for the ticket," Nicole said.

Robyn nodded vigorously.

They weren't kidding.

CHAPTER 2

Alex looked down at the boy waiting with her on the platform. He looked about eight years old and carried a small wooden shield painted gray with a yellow cross. His nose was smudged with dirt. No one else was standing in line to ride the elephant.

"Don't worry, lady."

"I'm not worried."

"Well, you should be!" The boy's eyes flashed as he pulled a toy wooden sword from a cardboard scabbard on his belt. "Dragons spit fire and bite!"

"Really?" Alex smiled and glanced at the massive elephant as it patiently plodded behind the woman handler. The animal looked totally bored and not at all dangerous. The boy was hardly a knight in shining armor, but his vivid imagination and serious manner were charming. It couldn't hurt to humor him.

"Real fire, huh?" Alex faked a worried frown.

"Yeah, but I'll protect you, lady."

"And just who are you, sir?"

"Penrod the Dragon Slayer." Scowling with menace, the boy glared at the elephant as it stopped on the far side of the platform.

Hiding an amused smile, Alex just nodded. Penrod probably wasn't the boy's real name. Members of the SCA gave themselves pretend names that fit their made-up Middle Ages identities.

Waving at Robyn and Nicole, Alex watched as an attendant wearing a turban, vest, and billowing pants with a bright orange sash helped four passengers out of the box-saddle. Then the handler moved the elephant into position in front of Alex and Penrod.

"Put the sword away, son," the attendant said as he opened the door on the box.

"How am I supposed to fight a dragon without my sword?" Penrod asked indignantly.

"You don't want to get thrown out of the fair, do you?"

"Better put it away." Alex didn't want Penrod to get into trouble because his enthusiasm overshadowed his better judgment.

Penrod set his jaw defiantly, but he slipped the toy blade back into its sheath and scrambled aboard. He sat down on the seat facing forward and crossed his arms.

"Make sure your brother behaves," the attendant warned Alex as she stepped into the box.

Taking the seat opposite Penrod, Alex tried to correct the man's false assumption. "He's not my—"

"Hey, Alex!" Robyn called out as the attendant latched the door and stepped back. "Smile!"

The box jolted as the elephant lumbered away from the platform. Gripping the side of the carrier with one hand, Alex waved with the other. Robyn took her picture while Nicole matched the elephant's pace on the far side of the fence.

"Robyn wants to get a shot of those acrobats!" Nicole gestured toward a grassy knoll. "Meet us over there when you're done!"

Alex nodded as Nicole and Robyn hurried away. From her vantage point on top of the elephant she could see through the trees and booths lining the path. Two men tossed a girl back and forth between them. The audience cheered the trio's aerial stunts. Alex watched in rapt fascination until her young companion suddenly went into action.

"Okay, dragon!" Eyes gleaming with mischief, Penrod drew his sword. "Prepare to defend yourself!"

"What are you doing?" Alex's stomach lurched as the box swayed with the motion of the elephant's walk.

"They don't call me Penrod the Dragon Slayer for nothing, lady."

Out of the corner of her eye, Alex saw the attendant watching them from the platform. If Penrod deliberately ignored the man's warning about the sword, they could both get kicked off the grounds. *Worse*, she realized as the box rocked and the boy started to stand up. Penrod could lose his balance and fall out.

"Sit down!" Alex said sharply.

"Make me!"

Alex frowned. Penrod was so caught up in the fair and his fantasy role playing, he didn't seem to understand that the danger was very real. The box-saddle tilted sharply to one side and Alex reacted instantly.

"I said *sit!*" Telekinetically yanking the sword

from the boy's hand, Alex pushed him back into his seat with an electromagnetic force field. Penrod gasped as his sword fell on the floor. Alex dragged it toward her with her foot and picked it up.

"How'd you do that?" Pinned by an invisible force, Penrod stared at Alex in astonishment.

"Do what?" Alex asked calmly, releasing him.

Shifting position, Penrod nervously averted his gaze. "Never mind."

Alex shrugged. Using her powers had not been smart, but she hadn't had much choice. The boy might have been seriously hurt. Besides, the jolting box could have made Penrod drop his sword and fall back into his seat. Judging by the boy's bewildered expression, that was exactly what he was thinking, too. He sat quietly for the rest of the ride.

"Ladies first." The attendant smiled as Alex stepped out of the box holding Penrod's sword.

Penrod jumped out behind her and darted across the platform.

"Don't forget your sword, Penrod."

Whirling, the boy grabbed it and scurried down the wooden stairs without looking back. He hit the ground running and disappeared into the trees.

Alex felt bad about bursting Penrod's make-believe bubble, but she knew she had done the right thing. He'd get over his wounded pride a lot faster than a broken bone from falling off an elephant.

Back on solid ground again, Alex put Penrod the defeated dragon slayer out of her mind and wove her way through the crowd and booths toward the knoll. After wandering for several minutes, she turned a corner and realized she had totally lost her sense of direction. A thick stand of dark woods bordered the dirt path on her left. The backs of log booths formed a wall on the right. Just ahead, a wooden signpost with gold lettering marked several converging trails.

Getting her bearings from the rustic sign, Alex turned to head back toward the center of the festival and stopped. On the trail in front of her, Penrod was talking to an older and much bigger boy. The teenager's arms, legs, and chest were wrapped with silver-coated padding held in place by buckles. A heavy bamboo stick dangled from his belt and a crude metal helmet was tucked under his arm. He carried a metal shield that resembled a battered garbage-can lid. The yellow cross painted on the dull gray surface was chipped and scraped. The older boy was obviously one of the combat contestants. It was easy to understand why Penrod had gotten so carried away with his dragon-slayer identity. He was probably too young to compete in the supervised games.

"That's her, Darian!" Penrod's eyes widened as he spotted Alex and pointed. "That's the sorceress!"

Sorceress? Alex froze as Darian slowly turned to regard her with a dark scowl.

CHAPTER 3

Alex stood her ground as the angry boy strode toward her with Penrod trotting at his heels.

"What did you do to my brother?"

Refusing to be intimidated by Darian's gruff and rude manner, Alex looked him in the eye. "Nothing. He was standing up on the elephant and I told him to sit down so he wouldn't get hurt."

"That's not how he tells it." Darian's cold, brooding eyes narrowed. His shoulder-length brown hair was matted and tangled from the helmet, and the grim set of his mouth made his angular face look too hard and callous for someone so young. "He says you pushed him and took his sword."

"She did, Darian!" Penrod hovered behind his brother. "But she didn't use her hands. It was magic!"

"So you say, brother."

Alex knew from talking with Robyn that many of the people acting out parts during the festival totally adopted their pretend personas. Obviously, Darian and Penrod did, too. Darian looked about sixteen—old enough to take care of himself and to know the difference between fantasy and reality. But he didn't seem to know that his little brother was taking his dragon-slayer role to a dangerous extreme.

"You don't honestly believe I used magic, do you?" Alex smiled, hoping the older boy would lighten up.

"Are you calling my brother a liar?" Placing his free hand on his bamboo stick, Darian eyed Alex intently.

"No," Alex said slowly, realizing that Darian's shield *was* a metal garbage-can lid. "He's just got a very active imagination. No insult was intended, sir."

"Sir? What kind of backward kingdom do you hail from?" Darian asked sarcastically. "I'm just a squire, not a knight. At least, not yet."

"But he will be," Penrod said. "After he beats Todd in the tournament. Then you can call him *Sir* Darian Gregor."

"That's nice. Now, if you'll excuse me—" As Alex stepped forward, Darian moved to block the path.

"A truly powerful sorceress is very rare. If I'm fighting as your champion in the tournament, Chadwick won't have a chance." Darian nodded as he studied her. "We must form an alliance."

Alex's patience with the game was wearing thin. Dressing up and getting into the spirit of the Renaissance Festival for fun was one thing. Darian's intensity was another. He gave her the feeling that his make-believe life as a wanna-be knight was more real and important to him than his regular life. That made her very uncomfortable. She wasn't worried that Darian would hurt her, but she was sure that if she encouraged the unfolding medieval drama, he would hassle her for the rest of the day. Alex just wanted to get back to her friends and her real life.

"Look, guys. I'm not a sorceress. I don't hail from a kingdom. I live in an ordinary town."

"So you're just a village peasant," Darian sneered.

Alex ignored the insult. "I'm a student working

on a history project with my friends, who are probably looking for me. Sorry, but I'm out of here.''

"I haven't given you leave to go!" Puffing out his chest, Darian silently dared her to pass.

"That's it." Spinning around, Alex quickly walked back the way she had come.

"How dare you!" Darian yelled.

When she was out of sight behind the log booths, Alex ducked into the woods and morphed. No sooner had she reduced herself to a puddle of silvery ooze than Darian and Penrod came charging around the corner of one of the log buildings. Hiding in the dense undergrowth, Alex listened and watched.

"Where'd she go?" Darian looked around in furious frustration as he skidded to a halt on the path.

Penrod shrugged. "I told you she was magic. She probably turned into a bird and flew away or something. Just like Merlin in King Arthur's court! Cool, huh?"

"No way, Penrod. A commoner can't defy a noble and get away with it." Jamming his helmet on his head, Darian stalked back toward the main grounds.

Penrod jogged to keep up. "If I were you, Darian, I'd leave her alone."

"Shut up, Penrod."

When they were gone, Alex slithered deeper into the woods. Far from curious eyes, she re-materialized in the cool shade of the towering trees. Sitting on a fallen log, she paused to consider her options. She didn't blame Penrod's impulsive nature or wild imagination for causing trouble with his older brother. It was her own fault for using her powers, which had seemed like magic to the boy.

Sighing, Alex started walking toward the sound of cheers and whistles. She couldn't change what had already happened, but she wasn't about to let Darian's distorted sense of reality ruin her day, either. He was determined to follow rules of behavior that were hundreds of years out of date. That, however, was his problem, not hers. The only solution to the unfortunate situation was to avoid him.

Staying in the woods, Alex headed toward the colored tents set up just beyond the trees near the competition field. The make-believe battles had started and it would be easy to lose herself among the spectators until she spotted one of her friends. The trees began to thin out and some boys were tossing leather balls on a strip of green grass to her right. Alex steered clear on the off chance Darian was one of several young men in armor watching the game.

She never saw the ball that hit her in the head and knocked her out cold.

She opened her eyes and stared into the leafy branches overhead. The ground was hard and a twig bit into her back. Pushing herself into a sitting position, she dropped her head into her hands as a wave of dizziness washed through her. When it passed, she touched the tender spot on her head and peered through the trees toward the fair.

A branch snapped.

A single thought flashed through her mind. Someone was looking for her, and that someone was dangerous.

"Excuse me."

She looked up to see a tall boy standing in the shadows a short distance away. Disoriented and alarmed, she lashed out with a fearful and powerful thought.

Get away from me!

The boy's eyes widened with shocked surprise as he suddenly stumbled backward and fell on the ground. He shook his head and flushed slightly with embarrassment.

She stared back as he brushed a stray lock of blond hair off his forehead and smiled. He wasn't the one.

"Some first impression! Stumbling over my own feet." Standing up, the boy brushed bits of leaves off his dark pants and the long sleeves of his open-necked white shirt. The silver studs on his leather breastplate and matching arm bands sparkled in a shaft of sunlight filtering through the trees. A leather scabbard decorated with colored stones and engraved silver inlays hung from his belt.

A warrior. She watched him warily.

"I'm Todd Chadwick." He took a step forward, then hesitated. "What's your name?"

She blinked. Her mind was a total blank.

"I don't know."

CHAPTER 4

She choked back a sudden rush of panic. She didn't know who she was or how she had knocked Todd to the ground just by thinking about it, but letting fear take control wouldn't help. Instinctively, she also knew it was safer to let him think he had stumbled.

Todd Chadwick, she thought as she started to rise. That name sounded familiar, but he didn't seem to know her.

"Here. Let me help you up." Todd held out his hand.

Taking it, she stood up and swayed slightly. She

pulled free when he tightened his grip to steady her. "Thanks, but I'm all right."

"I'm not so sure." Todd's blue eyes narrowed with concern. "You've got a nasty bump on your head and you don't know your own name."

"Uh—" She didn't think she had anything to fear from Todd, but she couldn't be certain. The feeling that someone was hunting her and that her life might be in danger was too strong to ignore, but she didn't have a clue who the someone was. She didn't have a clue about anything!

"I'm sorry." Holding up his palms, Todd backed away. "I didn't mean to be pushy. I thought you needed help."

"I do! Someone's chasing me."

She shuddered as a vague memory flashed through her mind. Her unknown enemy wanted to lock her away in an evil place forever. Wandering around the woods or the fair alone would not be safe. She had to trust her instincts about Todd. Still, she didn't think it would be wise to let him know she had lost her memory. He might want to take her to a first-aid station. It didn't make any sense, but the thought of seeing a doctor was terrifying.

"Who's chasing you?"

She shrugged helplessly.

"You really *are* in some kind of trouble, aren't you?"

"Uh, no—I mean, yes. I—" She exhaled slowly, determined to calm herself.

"Where are you from?"

"What kingdom?" She frowned. The word *kingdom* didn't seem right, and yet it had just popped out of her mouth.

"Kingdom? Oh, boy!" Todd laughed.

"Did I say something funny?"

"No, milady," Todd said, suddenly serious. "You are really good. This is the most intriguing plot I've ever stumbled into."

"It is?"

"It's brilliant! And daring, too." Todd grinned with animated enthusiasm. "Pretending to be lost with no memory of who you are or where you come from is a great idea, but anybody could have found you."

He thinks I'm acting! She wasn't sure why, but pretending to be pretending was the perfect solution to her immediate problem. She had had a couple of memory flashes within a few minutes. Maybe it wouldn't be long before she remembered everything. Until then, she needed the support of someone she could trust.

"What if the person who's after you had come along?" Todd raised an eyebrow and smiled slightly.

She realized he thought she had made up a villainous pursuer, too. She didn't blame him. It sounded too farfetched to be anything but a story.

"Or a dark knight with evil intentions?" Todd added.

A dark knight . . . A fleeting image of silver armor made her shift uncomfortably. There weren't any real knights anymore, and yet the threat from a dark knight felt real. Just as real as Todd's honest desire to help.

Heaving an exaggerated sigh, she lowered her eyes. "I am at your mercy, sir."

"Hardly. I've never been so enchanted by a girl that I tripped over my own feet before." Todd looked at her with a thoughtful frown, then winked. "Maybe you're a sorceress."

She looked up sharply. *Sorceress* . . . Like the image of the dark knight, the word aroused feelings of annoyance and dread. It also carried an essence of truth she did not understand. But the magical identity seemed to please Todd.

"A mysterious sorceress lost in the woods. Very cool."

She nodded silently. She wasn't sure how she had pushed him with her mind, but at least he didn't suspect.

"I am nothing but a lowly squire, milady, but my loyalty and services are yours to command." Todd bent forward in an elegant bow.

"Thank you." She smiled. In spite of her confusing and unnerving memory loss, she was starting to enjoy herself. For all she knew, her fear of being hunted by an evil enemy *was* part of a role-playing game.

"Come on then. I have to get back to help Sir Ravenwood prepare for his joust."

"Sir Ravenwood?" Shaking dry leaves off her dress, she followed as Todd led the way out of the woods.

"The knight who's sponsoring me. I've been his squire since I was thirteen. Three years now."

"What does a squire do exactly?" She wasn't asking just to be nice. She was genuinely interested.

Todd held a branch back to let her pass. "I clean

and repair his equipment and assist him in the jousts. And he teaches me everything I need to know to become a knight. And today just might be the day."

"That you'll become a knight?"

Todd shrugged as they stepped out of the trees into the sunshine. "Maybe. There are seven other squires in the tournament who want to be knighted as much as I do. Only one of us will win."

She nodded. Something about Todd and the tournament troubled her, too. The reason drifted in the darkness of her blocked memory, almost but not quite within grasp.

"Are you hungry?" Todd asked.

"Famished!" Fishing into her pocket, she drew out a wad of bills. "My treat. I insist."

Todd started to protest, then relented as he guided her toward a booth selling roasted turkey legs and fresh bread.

"I can't believe Alex got lost." Standing under the large tree in the clearing, Ray scanned the crowds.

"Me, neither." Robyn frowned. "Something must have happened to her."

"Not necessarily." Butter dripped down Louis's chin as he finished off his corn on the cob. "She's the one who was so excited about coming to this fair. She probably got distracted by a weaving demonstration or something."

"Weaving?" Nicole eyed Louis pointedly. "I don't think so."

"Okay, so weaving was a bad example, but you know what I mean. She's really into all this Middle Ages stuff." Rolling his eyes, Louis tossed the corn cob into a trash container and wiped his chin on the napkin Robyn handed him.

"Well, we've got to find her. She's been missing for over an hour." Ray was worried. They had checked with the elephant attendant before they came to the rendezvous spot by the tree. Alex had left right after the ride and she hadn't been seen since.

"Maybe *she* found someone." Louis rolled the napkin into a ball and threw it away.

"Like who?" Nicole asked.

"Prince Charming! Who else?" Shaking his head, Louis glanced at a young couple strolling by. "It has not escaped my attention that the girls here are nuts for guys wearing armor and those rattan practice swords."

"Not Alex's style, Louis," Ray said.

"And even if she had met someone, she wouldn't leave us hanging like this," Robyn said. "She knows I always think the worst."

"Well, I can't just stand here doing nothing." Ray looked at Robyn and Nicole. "You two check the lost and found and the first-aid station while Louis and I search the rest of the grounds. We'll meet back here in an hour."

"What if we don't find her?" Robyn asked.

"Let's worry about that in an hour." Ray didn't think Alex had run into ordinary trouble. He knew from experience that sometimes her powers went berserk. Maybe she was allergic to elephants. If something had suddenly made her start shooting super zappers or morphing uncontrollably, she'd be hiding on purpose, hoping he'd come looking for her. None of her other friends knew that Paradise Valley Chemical's experimental compound, GC-161, had turned Alex into a girl with extraordinary abilities.

After the girls left, Ray and Louis split up to search in opposite directions. Ray walked up and down every path, checking between booths and behind every tree. Alex wasn't anywhere. By the time he reached the tournament arena in the open field, he was getting frantic.

"Yo, Ray!"

Ray's heart jumped as Louis came up behind him. He turned and did a double take. Louis was wearing a headpiece made of connected metal rings called chain mail. A short sword made of heavy bamboo hung by a leather thong from his belt.

"Radical, huh?" Louis grinned sheepishly through the face opening in the linked metal circles that covered his head and part of his shoulders. "This medieval role-playing is pretty cool once you start to understand it. I was talking to this knight guy—"

"Louis!" Ray snapped. "You were supposed to be looking for Alex, not shopping."

"I know. She's over there. Hanging out with Prince Charming, just like I said." Louis pointed to the food booths near the corner of the arena.

Relief flooded Ray as he spotted Alex walking with a boy wearing silver-studded leather gear. His relief was instantly replaced by indignation. Alex and her new friend were both munching turkey legs and acting as though they didn't have a care in the world. She should have known he would be worried sick when she disappeared without a word.

"Alex!" Breaking into a run, Ray charged after them. "Alex! Wait!"

The boy in armor turned and frowned, then tapped Alex on the arm. Alex glanced back over her shoulder.

Ray stopped dead in his tracks, hurt and stunned as Alex did the one thing he didn't expect.

She took one look at him and ran the other way.

CHAPTER 5

Alex. . . .

She stopped and looked back, but the tall, dark boy had disappeared into the crowd.

Todd scowled darkly as his gaze swept over the festival crowd. "Was that who you were hiding from in the woods?"

"I don't think so." She sighed with frustration. Not being able to remember had made her too cautious and edgy. When she saw the tall boy running toward her, she had fled because she was startled. *Just like a scared rabbit flushed by a harmless noise*, she thought. That image did not appeal to her at all. Her memory was gone, but an innate sense of her inner self was becoming more clear. She was not a helpless damsel in distress. *And*, she silently vowed, *it's time I stopped acting like one.*

"So is he friend or foe?" Todd asked.

"Friend, I think." She smiled so Todd wouldn't realize how disturbed she really felt. Thinking about the tall boy didn't set off any alarms in her head. In fact, she had an unsettling suspicion that she knew him. Still, until she was positive he was not connected with the unknown danger looming over her, it was safer to keep her distance.

"Just when you think you know someone— *wham.*" Louis hustled to keep pace with Ray. "Alex is the last person in the world I expected to latch onto a knight."

"You're the one who thought that's what happened in the first place." Ray's cheeks burned with humiliation and hurt. Alex's rude behavior was like a slap in the face.

"Well, yeah. But I didn't really believe it." Louis's chain mail jingled as he jogged. "Can we slow down?"

"Sure." Sighing heavily, Ray paused by rows of wooden benches arranged in a shady glen. The forward section was filled with families waiting for the Punch and Judy puppet show to start. He sank onto an empty bench in the last row.

Dropping down beside him, Louis removed the metal headpiece. "Man, that thing's heavy! And hot! How'd anybody fight wearing a whole suit made of this stuff?"

"Why did you buy it?" Ray asked curiously, anxious to change the subject. He wondered if Alex realized how deeply she had hurt him. Or if she even cared.

"To improve my chances that one of these fair young maidens will fall for me." Louis shrugged with a lopsided grin, then nodded thoughtfully. "It's possible."

"You think so, huh?"

"Sure." Louis looked at him levelly. "If Alex can fall so hard for a guy wearing silver-studded leather that she doesn't want to be bothered with her friends, I know there's hope for me!"

Ray frowned. Louis had a point, but not the one he thought he had. Alex wasn't the kind of person who would develop an instant crush on a handsome stranger just because he was a knight. As Robyn said, even if Alex had met someone she liked, she wouldn't snub her friends.

Applause and cheers interrupted his thoughts as

the small curtain in the puppet theater parted and Punch and Judy popped onstage. Ray had seen the characters before, on a TV special about the art of puppeteering. Punch and Judy had a history that went back several hundred years.

"Cute," Louis said as Judy playfully tickled Punch with a flower to get him to wake up.

"Yeah." Ray's frown deepened. The original Punch and Judy had harassed and battered each other just like the Three Stooges. He understood that the puppets' violent behavior had been altered to protect the young audience, but the change had destroyed their unique identity. The two hand puppets looked like Punch and Judy in their colorful jester outfits, but since they didn't act like Punch and Judy, they weren't really Punch and Judy.

Alex wasn't acting like Alex, either.

"Do me a favor, Louis." Standing up, Ray backed off a few steps. "Find Robyn and Nicole and let them know that Alex is all right. There's no reason they shouldn't enjoy the fair on their own."

"What are you going to do?" Louis slipped his armor headpiece back on and adjusted it around his face

"I'll catch ya later." Ray left before Louis could

ask any more questions. Now that he had had a few minutes to think about Alex's strange behavior, he was sure there was a problem, and he couldn't risk letting Robyn, Nicole, or Louis find her in case the trouble involved her powers. Knowing Alex as well as he did, nothing else made sense.

"At least, now I know your name," Todd said as they hurried past tents and campsites on the far side of the tournament field. "Alex *is* your name, isn't it?"

"Yeah. It is." Alex brightened. Knowing her name hadn't triggered any other memories, but it was something. "I hope Sir Ravenwood isn't upset because you're late."

"We're not that late. Besides, I've got a good excuse. What kind of a knight would I be if I didn't take time to help a lady?"

Alex started to laugh. The sound died in her throat as Todd suddenly turned into a stand of trees.

"What do you think you're doing, Darian?" Todd strode forward to stand before a boy wearing silver-coated padding.

"None of your business, Chadwick."

Alex hung back, staring as an old man in a long robe reached for a lute the stocky boy held over his head. A battered garbage-can lid and a crude metal helmet were on the ground at the boy's feet.

The dark knight . . .

"Give Lyric his lute, Darian," Todd said evenly.

"You're such a bleeding heart, Chadwick," Darian sneered.

Alex's stomach twisted into a knot. She recognized that look. Darian was the one. Or was he? Her mind suddenly swam with a confused collage of faces and places: two men with short hair, older, one dressed in a blue uniform, the other with cold blue eyes . . . a stainless-steel lab stocked with delicate glass and metal equipment . . . a stylish woman with short, dark hair . . .

All of the images made Alex's heart flutter anxiously, but none of them had anything to do with the boy taunting the old minstrel.

"Please, Darian," the old man pleaded. "I've had that lute for over fifty years."

Laughing, Darian gripped the lute in both hands and fixed Todd with a piercing stare. "Think you can get to me before I smash it against this tree?" His dark eyes glinted, daring Todd to accept the cruel challenge.

Todd didn't move. He didn't dare, Alex realized, for fear Darian would destroy the delicate lute just to prove Todd couldn't stop him.

Alex felt her own fear dissolve in a surge of outrage. She didn't know why Darian was a threat to her and she didn't care. He was nothing but a bully.

Alex boldly stepped forward and glared at Darian. "Give it *back!*"

Darian's head snapped toward her as he threw the lute at the tree.

Horrified, Alex deflected the lute with her thoughts. It missed the tree and landed in Lyric's outstretched arms.

The old man held the lute protectively against his chest and gazed at Alex curiously.

A slow smile spread across Todd's face.

Alex's throat went dry. Her mind had grabbed the lute in midair and guided it toward the minstrel. She didn't need her own memory to know she shouldn't have been able to do that.

But she had.

Suddenly, Alex was no longer worried about who she was.

Now she had to worry about *what* she was!

CHAPTER 6

"You again!" Darian pivoted, flustered and furious. "Lucky for Lyric you startled me and ruined my aim!"

"Do you two know each other?" Surprised, Todd looked from one to the other.

Although her stomach was churning, Alex didn't flinch. None of them seemed to realize the lute had suddenly changed course.

"No, we don't. She gave Penrod a hard time this morning and I called her on it." Snatching up his dented shield and helmet, Darian glared at Alex. "This isn't the first time she's crossed me, but it better be the last!"

Alex stiffened as Darian turned and stomped off.

"That boy has a lot to learn." Lyric sighed, then smiled at Alex. "But knowing Penrod, I daresay he was up to some kind of mischief when you gave him a hard time."

Penrod. Alex suddenly remembered a small boy with a wooden sword. *The pint-sized dragon slayer.*

"He was going to fall," Alex said. "Off the dragon—uh, elephant."

"That sounds like Penrod." Todd shook his head, then clamped the old minstrel on the shoulder. "Are you okay?"

"Yes, I'm fine," Lyric said. "But you watch out for Darian in the tournament, Todd. Winning is more important to him than honor."

"It'll be a fair contest, Lyric."

"I'm sure it will—your side of it, anyway." Framed by long, white hair, Lyric's weathered face turned pensive. "Right now, though, I feel inspired to write a new ballad. About Todd and—"

"Alex." Todd glanced at Alex and whispered to the old man, "She's a sorceress."

"Of that I have no doubt. Anyone who can make Darian Gregor do her bidding on command must have magic powers." Strumming the lute and humming softly, the old minstrel wandered away.

Alex gasped softly, then quickly smiled to cover it. *Powers* . . . She didn't think the odd things she could do were magic, but they *were* a secret. A dark and burdensome secret she couldn't tell anyone, not even Todd and Lyric.

"Now we're late!" Waving Alex to follow, Todd jogged toward a blue-and-white tent set up on the outer edge of the camping area.

Alex skidded to a halt as Sir Ravenwood rose out of a high-backed chair to confront them. Standing six feet tall and wearing a blue-and-gold cloth coat of arms over a full suit of chain mail, the imposing man peered down at them. Alex's breath caught in her throat as she met the knight's penetrating gaze. Then he smiled.

"And who's this lovely lady, Todd?"

Beaming, Todd quickly explained. "I couldn't just leave her wandering around the woods alone."

"I should say not!" Sir Ravenwood laughed heartily, obviously amused and delighted with the story. After graciously extending his hospitality to Alex and instructing Todd to prepare his mount and lance, the knight left to check the demonstration schedule.

"He really does have a horse!" Alex stared at the huge animal tethered to a trailer parked behind the tent.

Todd grinned proudly. "My uncle's one of the best mounted knights in the country. He and his friends put on authentic jousting exhibitions at fairs all over the state."

"And you get to go with him?" Alex eased closer to the horse's head.

"Somebody's got to take care of Thunder." Todd laughed and patted the horse's sleek, reddish-brown flank.

Pulling hay from a hanging net, Thunder looked at Alex and snorted. She jumped.

"Don't worry, Alex. He's a warm-blood and the most sensible horse I've ever known."

"What's a warm-blood?" Alex cautiously extended her flattened hand and Thunder gently nuzzled her palm.

"A cross between a Thoroughbred and a draft horse." Todd opened a small door at the front of the trailer and pulled out a wooden box full of brushes and metal combs. "Those big draft horses were originally bred to carry knights wearing heavy armor. And they don't spook easily. It was very important to have a horse that didn't act nuts during a battle back then."

"I can imagine." Alex scratched Thunder behind the ears. "The Middle Ages were a lot more complex than I realized. I'm really impressed with how you and all these other people work so hard to keep the history alive."

"We try to uphold the nobler traditions." Todd stuffed a rag in his pocket, then muttered, "Most of us anyway."

Alex nodded. She knew exactly who he was talking about. "What is Darian's problem?"

Todd shrugged. "I honestly don't know. He takes the medieval codes of conduct so seriously, you think he'd have some sense of honor. But he just doesn't get it. Teasing Lyric is a perfect example."

"Yeah. I doubt that Lyric did anything awful to Darian. He seems like a really nice old man."

"He is, but there's more to it than that." Todd ran a brush over his hand to loosen the embedded dirt. "The ancient Celtic bards kept track of significant historical events with their songs. They could walk right through the middle of a battle without getting hurt by either side because everyone respected the importance of their work. Lyric does the same thing and he deserves the same respect."

Alex cocked her head. "Nobody ever attacked them?"

"Not even when the bard's songs made fun of them. If a song told about when someone did something stupid, and it was true, then that person had to live with being remembered for the mistake in a bard's epic poem." Todd grinned. "I bet that made a lot of people stop and think twice about doing something dumb."

"You really know a lot about this stuff, don't you?"

"Sorry." Todd blushed. "Sometimes I forget that everyone isn't as interested in history as I am. I didn't mean to bore you."

"I'm not bored. This is exactly what I wanted to find out when I came here today." Alex blinked, surprised by the unexpected flash of memory. She had come to the festival to learn about medieval times. It was a history project for school. Concentrating, she tried to recall faces, but all she remembered was fluzzy blurs. *At least*, she consoled herself, *I'm remembering something!*

Stepping back as Todd began to rub the horse's neck with a rubber currycomb, Alex almost tripped over Thunder's empty water bucket. "Does he need more water?"

"Yeah, he does."

"I'll get it." Alex picked up the bucket as Todd reached for the handle. "I want to help but I don't know anything about horses. I think I can manage to carry a bucket of water, though."

"Okay. Great. There's a water faucet over by the knights' staging area, but the creek is closer." Todd pointed to a path leading into the woods.

"I'll be right back." Swinging the bucket, Alex headed down the trail. Her mood darkened as the sunlight faded behind the canopy of leafy branches overhead. The dark and silent woods were an unnerving reminder of the silent darkness in her mind. The brief snatches of returned memory gave her hope, but so far the small bits of information hadn't helped much. Everyone went to school and the tall boy was probably one of her classmates. He couldn't be much of a friend, she decided. She was lost and he hadn't come after her when she ran. Of course, that also proved he wasn't an enemy, either. If she saw him again, it might be a good idea to talk to him. He might be able to fill in some of the blanks.

And there are a lot of blanks, Alex thought as she ducked under a low branch. The only thing she knew besides her name was that she could move things with her thoughts. And knowing that was not reassuring. It gave her the creeps. She didn't know how she knew, but the warnings in her mind were coming through loud and clear. The power was a secret that no one was supposed to know. The danger she felt was not a figment of her imagination. It was very, very real.

"Hold!"

Alex froze as Darian leaped out of the shadows into the path in front of her. Taking a deep breath, she ignored the trembling in her legs and matched his intense stare.

"What do you want, Darian?"

"You insulted me in front of my brother and shamed me in the eyes of that crazy old man. And then, after you refused my offer to form an alliance, you aligned yourself with Todd Chadwick, my archrival in the tournament!"

Alex stood quietly, letting Darian rant and rave. She didn't remember him asking her to be his ally, but he was upset to the point of being irrational. Maybe talking about what was bothering him would ease some of the tension.

"You owed my brother and his family a debt of honor, sorceress. I asked you to join us first." Planting his feet wide apart, Darian rested his hand on the hilt of his bamboo practice sword. "If you're going to play this game, you've got to play by the rules."

Remembering Todd's words, Alex faced Darian, feeling an odd mixture of annoyance and caution. Darian was serious about following the codes of conduct that governed society centuries ago. Too serious, she realized, and he only followed the rules that suited him.

"The rules say you can't hurt a minstrel," Alex said.

Darian squared his shoulders. "Lyric wrote a poem that called my shield a garbage-can lid."

"It *is* a garbage-can lid." The words were out of Alex's mouth before she could stop them.

"Another insult!" Darian's helmet visor fell over his eyes as he shook his dented shield.

In her mind Alex knew the gesture was just a display of frustrated anger, not an attack. But it took a second for that realization to register. By then, her defensive reflexes had already sprung into action.

Still clinging to the bucket with one hand, Alex threw out her other hand to protect herself.

And bolts of electricity shot from the tips of her fingers.

CHAPTER 7

The electrical bolt struck Darian's shield.

Alex jerked her hand back.

Darian yelped as his shield flew out of his hand. Flipping his visor up, he stared in white-faced shock. The metal disk banged on a rock, rolled on its rim, then fell over on the ground.

How did I do that? The question fled unanswered to the back of Alex's mind as she and Darian both looked up from the shield.

Their gazes locked.

Still stunned, Alex blinked. Had Darian been blinded by his visor? Or had he seen the golden electrical charge leap from her fingers?

A slow frown replaced the look of bewildered confusion on Darian's face.

Don't ever use your powers in public, Alex! The serious, worried face of a dark-haired girl flared in her mind. *They'll lock you up . . . lock you up . . .*

Alex turned and bolted into the woods with the unknown girl's warning hammering in her head.

The bucket bumped and rattled against her legs as Alex ran. Brush tangled around her feet, threatening to trip her. Startled birds took flight and small animals scampered out of her way. Her sleeve snagged on a branch and ripped as she pulled free. She ran on, driven by a single thought.

She had to get away from Darian. If he suspected she could do strange and amazing things and told anyone, her life—whatever it was—would be horribly changed forever.

Breathless and panicked, Alex stumbled to a halt on the bank of the creek. The bucket slipped from her hand as she stood, transfixed by a pool of clear water. Upstream, beyond the shallow pool created by a dam of soaked logs and branches, the water tumbled and gurgled over rocks.

Behind her, Darian crashed through the woods, hard on her trail.

The sparkling stream called to her.

Water.

Alex tensed as her toes and fingers began to tingle. The tingling sensation intensified, then suddenly rushed through her arms and legs, flooding her whole body with heat. Stricken as flesh and bone began to dissolve, Alex wondered for one brief, terrifying moment if her bizarre, unexplained powers had somehow overloaded her system and melted her. Or maybe a real sorcerer had cast an evil spell over her! That made as much sense as any other explanation.

Not that knowing why makes any difference now, Alex thought. Her body was disintegrating and there wasn't anything she could do to stop it. In the next agonizing moment, she shifted from being solid to being a tall pile of jelly to being a puddle of liquid ooze.

A puddle that could think and hear and see, Alex realized with amazed relief.

She saw the flash of silver armor through the trees and heard the metallic jingle and clank of buckles, shield, and helmet. She didn't have to think about what to do. She slithered into the shallow pool a split second before Darian stepped out of the woods.

Drifting just below the surface, Alex felt her fear

about turning into a puddle wash away. Being a liquid felt perfectly natural to her and not at all odd. She tried not to think about the possibility that maybe she couldn't turn back into her real self. She watched Darian instead.

Darian picked up the water bucket she had dropped and stared at it a moment. Then tossing it aside, he peered into the forest on the opposite bank and scowled. Exhaling loudly, he shook his head, then turned and trudged back into the woods toward the fairgrounds.

Wondering why Darian had given up so easily, Alex glided to the other side of the pool. When she looked up, she understood why he had not tried to pursue her deeper into the woods. A four-strand barbed-wire fence stretched along the far bank as far as she could see on both sides.

Afraid that Darian might come back, Alex decided to stay submerged a few minutes longer. Floating in the pool relaxed her and she was pretty sure Darian didn't know she could change into liquid ooze. If he did, he would have looked for her in the water. Besides, now that she had been a puddle for a couple of minutes, she was also certain she had morphed before and sooner or later she would change back into herself again.

Morphed. The term leaped out of the darkness, blocking the rest of her memory. It was a shortened form of another, much longer word the dark-haired girl used to describe the changing process. *Metamorphosed.* Alex suddenly felt like jumping for joy, but she couldn't because she didn't have legs. She dove and darted through the water instead. She didn't remember who the dark-haired girl was, but the girl knew about the odd powers and wanted to protect her from someone who wanted to lock her up.

Alex suddenly remembered the disturbing series of memory flashes she had when Darian was taunting Lyric. The woman with short hair and hard eyes filled her with dread.

She was the enemy.

Shrinking from the nameless woman's cold, calculating smile, Alex sank to the bottom of the pool. She settled on a bed of smooth rocks and gazed upward. Sunlight reflected off tiny motes of dirt suspended in the water, sparkling like a golden, underwater rain.

A rain of sticky gold gunk drenched her from head to toe.

Not a magic spell, Alex realized. It was worse. The snatch of memory was brief and fleeting like all the others, but it was a major clue. She had been exposed to some mysterious gold stuff. The weird powers were a result of the contamination. A shudder rippled through her, followed almost instantly by another warm tingling that coursed through her whole ooze-self.

Taken by surprise, Alex didn't react immediately. She suspected that she had had her powers for a long time. However, because she couldn't remember, she was learning about them as if it were the first time all over again. The tingling intensified. When she finally realized she was going to morph back into her normal solid form, it was too late.

A flash of heat flooded her as her cells suddenly shifted from liquid to solid and Alex re-materialized in the middle of the pool.

Water cascaded down her face. Alex sputtered as she pushed her long, dripping wet hair behind her ears. Then her boots slipped on the smooth rocks that had been a comforting cradle only seconds before. Swinging her arms to keep her balance, she stumbled toward the shore and fell onto the soft bank. Squishy mud splattered her arms, face, and hair.

Easing herself into a sitting position, Alex looked

down at herself and groaned. She could rinse the dirt off her skin and out of her hair, but her dress and boots were soaked and hopelessly streaked with mud and there was a huge tear in her sleeve.

Desperate and dirty, Alex sighed as she contemplated her predicament. She didn't need to remember to know that this was not turning out to be one of her better days.

Her memory was returning, but only in bits and pieces that were more confusing than not being able to remember at all. She couldn't deny that her powers were amazing, but they seemed to be more trouble than they were worth.

They were the reason the woman with the cold smile wanted to find her and lock her up.

And Alex was alone.

The worried dark-haired girl was just a nameless face in her mind and the tall, dark boy had disappeared. No one else seemed to be looking for her.

Even Todd was a total stranger, but right now he was the only friend she had in the world.

CHAPTER 8

Ray stared at the ground as he waited for Louis to pay for his hot apple turnover. He wasn't hungry. He had joined Louis, Nicole, and Robyn after searching the festival a second time, but he hadn't spotted Alex again. The only place he hadn't looked was the contestants' camp on the far side of the arena. Spectators weren't allowed behind the scenes unless they were with a participant. He wondered if Alex was there with her new friend. The restricted area would be a great place to hide if she was in trouble.

Except for one thing, Ray thought. Why would Alex turn to a stranger for help and avoid him— her best friend?

Apple juice squished out the corners of Louis's mouth as he took a bite of the steaming pastry. He chewed, swallowed, and smiled with satisfaction. "That's good."

Robyn and Nicole exchanged amused glances as they all started toward the jousting field.

"You haven't stopped eating since we got here, Louis," Robyn said.

Nicole teased him. "If our history report were about medieval food, we'd be a shoo-in for an A."

Following behind the others, Ray smiled in spite of his worry about Alex. For someone who thought attending a medieval fair was a dull way to spend a Saturday, Louis had really gotten into the spirit of the event.

"Don't worry about that A," Louis said confidently. "I've learned a lot. Did you know those knight guys used to joust to decide who was right and who was wrong?"

Robyn nodded. "Trial by combat. They believed that whoever was right would win *because* they were right."

Nicole frowned thoughtfully. "So even if someone was actually guilty, all he had to do was win a fight to get off the hook?"

"Yeah." Louis adjusted the chain-mail headpiece under his chin. "Cool, huh?"

"For the big guys, maybe," Nicole said. "If you ask me, it was a totally unfair justice system. I mean, what about women? They weren't allowed to fight. What did they do when they were accused of something?"

"They got a knight to fight for them." Louis winked. "As their champion."

Nicole rolled her eyes. "I think I'd rather fight my own battles."

"Me too," Robyn agreed, "but medieval women didn't exactly have a choice. They didn't have any more freedom than the peasants. Still—" She sighed wistfully. "There is something incredibly romantic about having a knight defend your honor. It's easy to understand why some of these people like to pretend it's real for a few days."

Ray looked up sharply. Maybe Alex had gotten involved in a role-playing game. That was something he hadn't considered before. Alex had suggested the Middle Ages for their group history project because she was fascinated by medieval society. Role playing would be a great way to learn and he had seen her with a boy dressed in leather armor who probably belonged to the SCA.

"Pictures of the horseback jousts will be super for our report, Robyn," Louis said enthusiastically.

"The guys who put on these exhibitions are almost like the real thing."

"I know. Everybody's talking about the mounted demonstrations." Robyn frowned at the camera. "I've only got a couple of shots left on this roll, though. I should use them up and start a new roll before the jousts start."

Louis struck a dramatic pose, putting one hand on his hip and the other on his wooden sword. "Snap away."

Robyn eyed him uncertainly, then shrugged and raised the camera.

Nicole walked on ahead with Ray. "When is Alex going to meet us? She's been gone an awfully long time."

"Uh—" Ray coughed, thinking fast. He had thought of a dozen reasons why Alex might have disappeared, but they were only guesses. He still didn't know if she was having power problems. "She didn't say exactly, but she's, uh—doing some really cool research."

"Well, I wish she'd clue us in, Ray. This is supposed to be a group project."

"Look! Aren't they great?" Louis ran past, pointing toward the field.

The mounted jousting exhibition hadn't started

yet, but two boys were walking costumed horses on the field. Colored cloths with scalloped edges covered the breastplates and reins. The saddles were draped with bigger cloths bearing each knight's coat of arms.

Nicole forgot about Alex as she pressed toward the roped-off field with Louis and Robyn.

Ray couldn't forget her. Something wasn't right and he couldn't relax until he found out what. "I need something to drink. Anyone want anything?"

Robyn and Nicole shook their heads. Louis was so engrossed in joust preparations, he didn't seem to hear.

Ray quickly slipped away. If he couldn't find Alex, maybe he could find her silver-studded knight.

Todd finished cinching Thunder's saddle, then smoothed Sir Ravenwood's coat-of-arms blanket over it. He turned and stared as Alex trudged up to the trailer. "What happened?"

Setting the full water bucket in front of the horse, Alex sighed. Leaves stuck to her damp, torn, muddy dress and her boots were coated with dirt. Her tangled, wet hair was plastered to her head. She looked more like a peasant who had just finished feeding the pigs than she did a lady. It was embarrassing enough having to face Todd, but then Sir Ravenwood strode around the side of the tent to join them.

"My dear Lady Alex," the knight said gently. "What grave misfortune has befallen you?"

"I fell in the creek." Alex crossed her arms self-consciously, covering the tear in her sleeve with her hand.

"And what were you doing by the creek?"

"Getting water for Thunder. I wanted to help."

"I see you accomplished your quest." Sir Ravenwood glanced at the bucket. "And at great peril, too."

Alex shrugged. She didn't mind the knight's teasing. Even if she could tell the truth, Todd and Sir Ravenwood would never believe she had gotten soaked because she didn't get out of the water before she changed from a puddle back into a girl. In a way, though, her bedraggled appearance was an advantage. Now she had a good excuse to stay away from the joust arena. Darian would probably be there, and she did not want to run into him again.

"I, uh—don't think I'll be able to watch you joust, Sir Ravenwood. I really wanted to, but I'm such a mess."

Todd looked at his uncle. "There must be something we can do."

"Yes, there is." Scowling, Sir Ravenwood called to Todd over his shoulder as he walked away. "Finish tacking up Thunder. I'm facing Sir Henry in the first round."

Alex sagged against the side of the trailer, feeling like a total dork.

Todd glanced at her and smiled as he lifted a bridle off a hook. "You're still the prettiest girl here."

"I don't know about that, but I'm certainly the clumsiest." Alex grinned. "I probably tripped over *my* own feet and knocked myself out in the woods, too."

Todd eyed her curiously. "Knocked yourself out? You mean for real?"

"Uh—" Alex faltered, fumbling for an explanation to cover her slip. Todd thought she was pretending to be lost and unable to remember anything. "Just dazed myself a bit. Nothing serious."

Afraid of saying something else she shouldn't, Alex watched quietly as Todd slipped the reins over the horse's head and unbuckled the halter. In one fluid movement, he eased the bit between

Thunder's teeth and slipped a leather strap over his ears.

"Doesn't wearing all that stuff bother him?" Alex was interested and talking about the horse distracted her from her own dire problems.

"Not at all." Holding the reins together under Thunder's chin, Todd backed him up. "To be honest, I think he likes dressing up and charging full tilt at another horse and rider as much as my uncle does. It's in their blood."

"Sounds dangerous."

"It would be if they were using real lances." Todd nodded toward several long poles leaning against a metal rack. "Those are made of flexible plastic with eighteen-inch sponge tips. Even so, I'm not ready to try it, yet."

"Do you ride?"

Todd nodded brightly. "Whenever my uncle lets me."

As Todd led Thunder away, Alex followed and studied the huge horse in awe. She couldn't imagine anyone being able to control such a powerful animal.

"Ah, there you are, Lady Alex." Standing in front of his high-backed chair, Sir Ravenwood bowed his head smartly as Alex stepped into view.

"I have something for you. For services rendered to this humble knight."

Alex glanced at Todd.

Todd shrugged.

Grinning, Sir Ravenwood moved aside.

Alex stared in openmouthed wonder and delight. A long crimson dress was draped over the back of the chair. The V-shaped neckline, high waist, and hem were trimmed in elegant black lace. White lace flowers adorned the front and the long sleeves that tapered to points at the wrists. A crown of pink and yellow flowers was looped over the chair arm and a pair of black leather slippers rested on the ground.

"It's beautiful." Alex gently ran her hand over the velvety fabric. "Where did you get it?"

Sir Ravenwood sighed. "Now that my daughter's in medical school, she doesn't have time to dress up and play princess with her father. I've lugged a trunk full of her costumes around for years—for sentimental reasons." The knight smiled and winked. "But there's no sense letting them sit around gathering dust. This one's yours now."

"You're giving it to me?" Alex was stunned. "Thank you. I don't know what to say."

"The look on your face says it all, milady." Taking Thunder's reins from Todd, Sir Ravenwood swung into the saddle. "You must hurry and change so you don't miss the joust. My shield, Todd!"

"Yes, m'lord." Todd grabbed a shield decorated with an intricately painted coat of arms from where it leaned against the tent, and handed it to the knight.

"And the lances!" Sir Ravenwood boomed, then urged Thunder into a brisk trot toward the arena.

"See you in a few minutes, Alex." Collecting three lances, Todd ran after his uncle.

When they were gone, Alex carefully carried the dress, shoes, and floral crown into the tent and paused. Suitcases and duffles heaped with regular and medieval clothes were piled on the floor with an assortment of shields, gloves, chain-mail head-pieces, helmets, and swords. A camping lantern sat on a small table. Two cots lined opposite sides of the canvas shelter. A leather shield inlaid with en-graved silver strips and silver studs leaned against one of the cots. Matching arm and leg coverings, a helmet, and a wooden short sword in a leather scabbard tooled with a delicate scroll pattern were carefully arranged on top of it.

Todd's combat armor, Alex thought as she placed

her new clothes on the empty end of the other cot. All Todd's leather had been recently buffed and polished and the silver ornamentation gleamed. Like his uncle, he obviously took good care of and great pride in his equipment.

As Alex started to untie the neck of her ruined T-dress, she caught sight of herself in a small mirror. Her damp, snarled hair was a fright. She desperately needed a comb, but it wouldn't be polite to use Todd's or Sir Ravenwood's without permission. *But Thunder won't mind if I borrow one of his!*

Alex dashed out to the horse trailer and rummaged in the grooming box until she found a mane comb that looked practically new. She felt bad about missing Sir Ravenwood's jousting demonstration, especially since he had been so kind and generous. *But at least I'll look presentable when he and Todd come back.*

Alex couldn't wait to change into the elegant gown, but she didn't want to use the horse's comb on her hair without rinsing it off. But Thunder had drunk from the water bucket and she wasn't thrilled about returning to the creek. Then she remembered the water faucet Todd had pointed out.

Alex wasn't thrilled about being seen in her

dirty, torn T-dress, either, and took a roundabout route. She just barely avoided being spotted by Darian as he headed in the opposite direction, his eyes darting furtively from side to side. Watching from behind an elaborately decorated tent, Alex shuddered. Darian seemed to be looking for trouble and she was glad he wasn't going to find her.

Anxious to get back to the tent, Alex ran water over the comb and rubbed it clean with her fingers. Then, needing the water to loosen her drying snarls, she stayed by the faucet until the wide-toothed comb ran smoothly through her long hair. She kept an eye out for Darian as she hurried back to the camp site, but she didn't see him anywhere.

Then, as she dropped Thunder's comb back into the grooming box, she found out why.

A ripping noise inside the tent put Alex instantly on the alert. Quietly easing back between the tent and the horse trailer, she listened. The jingling of buckles and Darian's voice were unmistakable.

"That'll fix you, Todd."

Alex didn't know what Darian was up to, but it couldn't be good for Todd. Confronting the sullen boy wouldn't be good for her. Darian was already too hostile.

But she had to do something.

Why can't I use my astounding powers to get Darian out of Sir Ravenwood's tent?

No reason, Alex thought as she silently moved to the back of the horse trailer. *As long as nobody sees me.*

The loading ramp was down. Ducking inside, Alex concentrated on the ramp. The platform slowly raised off the ground, powered by her thoughts. The hinges squeaked softly and she almost dropped it before the metal catches clicked into place. Shifting her focus, she telekinetically found the outside pins and "thought" them through holes in the clasps.

With the ramp secured, she peered through the air vent at the front of the right-hand stall. Squinting, she focused on the box of grooming tools below. A stiff brush rose easily into the air. Projecting another powerful thought, she hurled it at the tent.

Thump!

Inside, Darian grunted with surprise.

Throwing the brushes with her mind was second-nature once Alex let herself go. A barrage of thuds and thumps sounded as the tools hit taut canvas one after another.

Darian ran out through the front flaps and

stormed to the back of the tent. He stopped dead, obviously expecting to find the person throwing things and surprised to find the area deserted. Scowling, he walked to the back of the trailer.

Alex crouched down. The space between the top of the trailer and the raised ramp was only six inches wide and the pins were fastened on the outside. As she expected, Darian looked and left. To all appearances, there was no way a person could be hiding in the locked horse trailer.

Not an ordinary person anyway, Alex thought.

After cautiously looking through the forward vent to make sure Darian was gone, Alex telekinetically unlocked the ramp and lowered it. She raced inside the tent and stopped dead in her tracks.

Darian had sabotaged Todd's beautiful leather armor.

CHAPTER 9

Getting more worried with each passing minute, Ray felt a rush of relief when he finally spotted Alex's new friend on the far side of the arena. Ray frowned as the boy handed a lance to one of the mounted knights, then moved back to wait with several other boys. Alex wasn't with him, but Ray was sure he knew where she was. The problem was getting near the boy to ask.

Men dressed as royal guards were patrolling a sawhorse barrier that had been set up to keep casual curiosity seekers out of the camp and away from the knights' staging area. Ray's heart sank as he watched them turn away a distinguished-looking man with a camera. They weren't going to let him walk through, either.

Not unless he had a good reason for being there.

The sun was high in the sky and it was getting hot. Realizing he really was thirsty, Ray skirted the large crowd gathering to watch the jousts and headed toward the nearest vendor selling drinks. Maybe soothing his parched throat with a cool lemonade would clear his head so he could think straight. There had to be some way to get past the guards.

Keeping an eye on Alex's friend, Ray stood at the end of the long line. He felt sorry for the knights. They had to be sweltering in their heavy metal armor—

Ray blinked. The boys assisting the knights were probably hot and thirsty, too. Fishing into his pocket, Ray counted his money. He had more than enough to buy small drinks for the knights' helpers. The guards might just let him pass if he was carrying a cardboard tray. It was worth a shot and he didn't have any other bright ideas.

Waiting anxiously as the line inched forward, Ray stood so he could watch the arena.

"It's about time!" Holding a wooden shield and sword, the small boy in front of Ray huffed impatiently as he stepped up to the counter. A larger boy dressed in silver-coated padded armor rushed up to join him.

"Get me one, too, Penrod." Sweating and out of breath, the older boy handed Penrod a dollar bill.

"Two lemonades." Penrod put the money on the counter and glanced at the bigger boy. "Have you seen that magic girl again, Darian?"

Ray stiffened. *Magic girl?* Trying not to be too obvious about it, he listened with mounting apprehension.

"Stay away from her, Penrod."

"Why? She wasn't mean or anything and I think it would be neat to have a sorceress for a friend."

"She's not a sorceress."

"Yes, she is!" Penrod said stubbornly. "She pushed me and took my sword without using her hands."

"Right." Darian sighed as he leaned down and hissed at Penrod. "Believe what you want, Penrod, but she's no friend of ours. She insulted us and that makes her the enemy."

Penrod's face darkened unhappily. "Aw, Darian."

Ray's heart began to pound and the palms of his hands got clammy. He was sure the boys were talking about Alex. He was also positive something was very, very wrong. Alex would never use her powers in public unless there was a terrible problem and she had no choice. Even then, she was usually careful to make sure no one realized she was doing anything strange. Why had she been so careless in front of this boy called Penrod?

Darian's eyes narrowed angrily. "And she's joined forces with Todd Chadwick."

"Oh." Penrod sighed as he picked up the drinks and handed one to Darian. "That's too bad."

"For her. She should have taken my offer to form an alliance when she had the chance, but it's too late now. When the competition's over, Todd will still be a squire and I'll be a knight." Darian nodded with a sly grin and glanced toward the arena. "He's gonna lose."

"I wouldn't count on that," Penrod said solemnly. "Todd's really good."

Darian averted his gaze and shifted uncomfortably. Then he and Penrod started walking away. "Not good enough to handle what I've got in store for him."

Stunned, Ray just stood staring into space.

"Can I help you?" The woman behind the counter bent forward, raising her voice.

"Uh—yeah." Ray fumbled in his pocket for his money. "Six lemonades and something to carry them in, please."

With the cardboard tray of drinks in his hands, Ray hurried toward the barricade. His head was spinning. Everything he had thought of that could possibly explain Alex's absence seemed to be true, if Darian and Penrod's conversation was accurate. She had gotten herself in the middle of a rivalry between her new friend, Todd, and Darian. And either she couldn't control her powers or circumstances had forced her to use them. The sooner he found her, the sooner he'd know exactly what the problem was.

Keeping a steady pace, Ray smiled and nodded at the guard by the sawhorses as he began to walk through the open space in the barrier.

"Whoa, there, son. Where are you going?"

Ray looked back as though the question came as a surprise. "I'm taking these drinks to Todd Chadwick and his friends. Over there." He lifted his elbow to motion toward the group standing near the arena entrance. "Squires get thirsty, too," he added when the guard frowned uncertainly.

"That they do, son. That they do." The man waved him on. "Get on with ye, then."

"Thanks." Moving quickly, Ray hustled toward the squires as two knights entered the arena and took positions on opposite ends. The dappled gray horse on the far side reared. The crowd cheered and whistled. The knight on the black horse close to the gate kept his mount perfectly still as they faced off. Ray hung back as the squires surged toward the ropes to watch.

"Galahad's sure feeling his oats today," one of the boys said as the gray horse wheeled on his back legs.

"Sir Ronald likes to put on a good show," another boy said with a smile.

Ray eased up next to Todd as the marshall supervising the joust raised his hand, then dropped his arm. Both riders charged forward, leveling their long lances. Galahad shied to the side slightly as they passed and Sir Ronald's sponge-tipped lance just grazed the black knight's armor. The black knight's lance hit Sir Ronald's chest armor squarely. The force was not enough to unseat the knight on the skittish gray horse, but the man on the black horse was awarded the point. They continued on across the arena, then turned and prepared for a second charge.

Todd looked back over his shoulder, then

frowned when he noticed Ray standing beside him. A flicker of recognition flashed in his eyes. "How'd you get in here?"

"I had to talk to you, Todd." Ray met Todd's wary gaze with a direct, no-nonsense stare. "About Alex."

"What about Alex?" Todd eyed Ray suspiciously.

Sensing that Todd's reaction seemed more protective of Alex than hostile toward him, Ray spoke in a rush. "I'm Ray Alvarado. I've been Alex's best friend since I almost ran into her with my tricycle when we were four years old. She came here with me and some friends to research a school project, but then she disappeared. That was hours ago and the only time I've seen her since then, she was with you."

"A school project?" Todd cocked his head. "She's not from one of the other SCA kingdoms in the state?"

Ray started slightly. "No. She's from Paradise Valley. And to be honest, it's not like her to run off without saying anything to anybody. I've been worried sick about her."

Todd studied Ray intently for a long moment, then nodded. "You really are worried, aren't you?"

"She's my best friend."

"Todd!" A mounted knight's deep voice thundered. "Another lance, if you please."

"Be right back. Don't leave." Todd grabbed a lance from a rack and ran toward the man.

Ray looked toward the other squires. "Lemonade, anyone?" The boys eagerly accepted his drinks and welcomed him into the group.

"What's the problem?" one of the boys asked when Todd returned a few minutes later.

Shaking his head, Todd held up a lance with a bent sponge tip. "Sir Ravenwood fought a gallant battle with a tree when he was practicing."

Ray laughed with the others, but he was getting more and more anxious about Alex. "I know you're busy, Todd, but I have to find Alex."

"I expected her to be here by now. She really wanted to see the jousts." Todd sighed and looked toward the arena as Sir Ravenwood rode Thunder to the far end. "I have to stay until my uncle's finished. If Alex doesn't show by then, I'll take you to her."

"Thanks." Relaxing, Ray edged toward the ropes to watch Sir Ravenwood. His opponent, Sir Henry, was also riding a big brown horse with a black mane and tail. However, the resemblance stopped there. Although Thunder snorted and pawed the ground while he waited, the other horse pranced nervously.

Across the arena, Ray spotted his other friends. Robyn was busy snapping pictures and Nicole and Louis were cheering enthusiastically. They seemed to be totally entranced by the spectacular demonstration. Ray didn't think they'd miss him for a while, yet.

Thunder never flinched as Sir Ravenwood urged him into a gallop beside the short wooden posts lined up to separate the two riders. On the first pass, Sir Henry's lance was too low and snagged on the fence. Sir Ravenwood made solid contact with Sir Henry's armor. In the end, Todd's uncle won all four passes and the match.

"He won't have to ride again until this evening after the knighthood competition," Todd explained as he led Sir Ravenwood's horse through the camp.

"And you're fighting in that, right?" Ray carried the knight's three lances. In spite of Todd's assurances that Thunder was the most trustworthy horse at the festival, Ray kept a respectable distance. Thunder was big.

"It's not really a fight. More like a demonstration of ability. We're only allowed to strike shields and our opponent's padded chest, arms, and legs. And we have to control the force of our blows or we get points taken off."

"Points?" Ray asked, confused. "Doesn't the winner of the tournament automatically get to be a knight?"

"Usually. Combat skills count for fifty percent of the points. The knights also judge us on equipment, which we have to make ourselves, and sportsmanship."

Ray nodded. After he cleared things up with Alex, he wanted Louis to meet Todd. There was more to being an SCA knight than wearing chain mail and carrying a wooden sword.

"Alex!" Todd called out as he stopped by the horse trailer. Looping the reins over his arm, he slipped the coat-of-arms sheet off the saddle, then unbuckled the cinch.

"Maybe she's not here." Ray leaned the lances against a rack holding several others.

"Then she didn't go far." Pulling the saddle off Thunder's back, Todd placed it on a wooden rack shaped like a wedge. Then he removed the bridle, strapped on the horse's halter, and clipped a leather lead shank to a ring under Thunder's chin. "Alex?"

"Over here!"

Ray grinned at the sound of Alex's voice coming from the tent. She wasn't hurt, so whatever else was going on couldn't be too bad.

Todd dropped a big sponge in the water bucket and picked the bucket up. Leading the horse, he motioned Ray toward the front of the tent. He stopped abruptly, eyes widening when he saw Alex framed in the canvas-flap opening. "Wow!"

Alex hesitated uncertainly, staring at Todd.

Ray stared at the beautiful girl in the long red dress with the high, fitted waistline. A flowered wreath held her long, light brown hair in place. She sure didn't look like the Alex with scraped knees, dirt-smudged face, and knotted braids who used to play with him in the backyard sandbox.

"What happened to the dress you made?" Ray asked.

A look of sheer terror flashed across Alex's face as she gasped and turned toward him. "Do I know you?"

"Know me?" Stricken, Ray glanced at Todd.

Setting down the bucket, Todd pulled out the dripping sponge and began to wash the sweat off Thunder's hide. "I know how easy it is to get carried away with a story and a make-believe identity, Alex, but you really should have told Ray what you were up to. It wasn't very cool to worry your best friend. He's been looking for you all day."

"So this is a role-playing thing." Exhaling, Ray stared at the ground for a moment. He was angry now and couldn't hide it. He wasn't mad because Alex had adopted a pretend personality for the day. He was upset because she hadn't included him. His day had been ruined because he had spent all his time worrying and searching for her. He looked up and glared. "So who are you supposed to be?"

Alex's mouth fell open but no words came out. She desperately looked back and forth between the two boys.

"Actually, it's pretty clever." Tossing the sponge in the bucket, Todd began to walk Thunder in a wide circle. "I found her wandering around the woods pretending to be a lost sorceress."

"A sorceress!" Ray snapped. He couldn't believe Alex was using her powers to support a stupid medieval identity to impress Todd and a little boy.

"Who lost her memory," Todd explained. "It's one of the best role-playing ideas I've ever heard."

"I'm not playing," Alex said.

Ray raised a skeptical eyebrow.

Todd stopped walking the horse and just stared at her.

Taking a deep breath, Alex regarded Todd steadily. "I really don't remember anything." Her gaze flicked to Ray. "Or anyone."

CHAPTER 10

Alex watched Ray anxiously. He did look familiar, but her mind was still only a blur of vague and confusing recollections. If the tall boy was really her best friend, why didn't she remember him?

"You mean you've *really* lost your memory?" Todd asked.

Alex nodded. "I know it sounds ridiculous, but I honestly don't remember much of anything. I've had a few flashes, but for the most part, my mind's a complete blank."

"You're not kidding, are you?" Ray's angry, doubtful expression instantly changed to concern. "Well, that sure explains a lot."

Like what? Alex wanted to ask, but she didn't. Although she had decided earlier it might be a good idea to talk to Ray, right now Todd's problem was more important.

"Todd, there's something—"

"How did this happen, Alex?" Ray rushed to her side and guided her to Sir Ravenwood's chair. "Sit down."

"I'm not sure." Alex answered as she sat, then turned back to Todd, who was pacing and leading Thunder. "Todd—"

Todd looked up suddenly. "You said you tripped and knocked yourself out in the woods, remember? I bet that's how you lost your memory."

"That sounds reasonable," Ray said.

Todd's face grew serious. "I think we'd better get you to the first-aid tent right away. There's a doctor—"

"No!" Alex and Ray shouted in unison, then exchanged questioning glances.

"Why not?"

"Uh—because—she—she—uh—just—can't go—" Ray stammered.

Alex's heart flip-flopped as she recalled how the idea of seeing a doctor had frightened her when

Todd found her in the woods. Apparently, Ray knew why, but she could ask him about that later.

"Because we don't have time," Alex said as Todd continued to walk the horse. "Could you stand still for a minute, Todd? This is really important."

Todd paused to touch Thunder's chest and behind his ears. "Nope. He's still hot. It may take another half hour to finish cooling him out."

"Huh?" Again Alex and Ray responded together, equally bewildered.

"When a horse gets overheated from a heavy workout," Todd explained patiently, "you've got to keep him walking until he cools down or he'll get sick."

"Oh." Ray nodded, but he still looked confused.

Alex jumped up and held out her hand. "I'll do it. You'd better go look at your equipment. It's not in the same condition it was when you left."

Todd paled as he handed Alex the leather lead and sprang for the tent. "Don't let him drink any water."

"Okay." Alex slumped, feeling slightly nauseated. That was just how Todd would feel when he found his armor strewn around the tent with torn leather straps and ripped-off silver studs piled on the floor. She hadn't moved anything because she wanted him to see exactly what Darian had done.

Holding one hand close to the halter clip, Alex hitched her long skirt off the ground and clutched the end of the leather strap. Tugging on the lead, Alex started walking. "Come on, Thunder."

The horse followed obediently.

"Careful, Alex," Ray cautioned. "He's a lot bigger than you are."

Alex nodded. She walked with the horse's head at her side as Todd had done. When Thunder nudged her arm with his nose, she gently nudged back and he moved away. The massive animal was surprisingly easy to handle.

Hanging away a few feet, Ray walked with her. "Have you noticed that you can do some—uh, really weird things—like shooting electricity out of your fingers?"

Stricken, Alex stared at him.

"Guess you have," Ray said, noticing her expression. "You've got to stop using your powers like magic in front of people, Alex, or you're going to be in more trouble than you can imagine. I heard—"

"How do you know about that?" Alex gasped. "Nobody's supposed to know!"

"Exactly. Nobody knows except you, me, and Annie."

"Annie—" Alex paused, turning the name over in her mind as she turned the horse to head back toward the tent. The dark-haired girl . . . *is my older sister, who'll have a royal fit if she finds out I used my powers in public!* Ray didn't look too happy, either.

"I didn't mean to, Ray. They just—happened before I even knew I had them!" Alex was suddenly aware that having Ray nearby was very comforting. He cared about her and he knew about her powers. So she and Annie, the older sister she barely remembered, obviously trusted him enough to keep the dangerous secret.

"Maybe you should tell me what you do remember, then I can fill in the important stuff until—" Ray stopped talking as Todd trudged out of the tent.

"What happened?" Todd asked softly, looking at Alex.

"That's what I was going to ask you," Ray said.

"Someone tried to demolish my armor," Todd said, dazed.

"Darian," Alex said simply. "He was inside when I got back from the water faucet a little while ago. I threw things at the tent and chased him off, but I didn't get here in time to stop him. I'm so sorry."

"You shouldn't have done that, Alex. Darian isn't exactly a friend of yours after you embarrassed him in front of Lyric."

"He didn't see me."

"Darian?" Ray's eyes narrowed. "The guy wearing armor that makes him look like the Tin Man from *The Wizard of Oz?*"

Todd laughed in spite of his misfortune. "The same. But don't say that to his face."

"Or call his shield a garbage-can lid," Alex added as she urged Thunder back into a walk.

"Even though it is." Sighing, Todd got to his feet and ran his hand through his hair. "My armor problem isn't just that equipment counts for twenty-five percent of the points. We can't compete in the combat part without protective gear that's functional. All my straps are ruined."

"I heard Darian talking at the lemonade stand," Ray said. "He said you wouldn't be able to handle what he had in store for you. Now I know what he meant. I'm a witness and so is Alex. Can't you turn him in to the knight cops or something?"

Todd shrugged. "I could, but I'm not going to."

"You're not?" Alex asked.

"No. I'd rather meet him face to face on the field like a real knight. Trial by combat. I have to believe that justice and honor will win."

Alex nodded.

Ray clamped a hand on Todd's shoulder. "That right-is-might stuff doesn't make any sense at all, you know. But in a weird way, I believe it, too."

Smiling, Todd walked to Thunder to see if he was still overheated. "Do you mind walking him some more, Alex?"

"No. Not at all." Alex grinned and patted Thunder's neck. "I'm getting to like him."

"Thanks. Maybe I can salvage some of my stuff if I get to work right away."

"How bad is it?" Ray asked as he followed Todd to the tent.

"Nothing I can't fix if I have enough time."

"Could you use some help?" Ray asked. "I don't know anything about leather armor, but I'd like to pitch in. I've got three other friends here who'd love to get behind the scenes and lend a hand, too. It'll be dynamite research for our school project."

"Sure!" Todd's gloomy face brightened. "It doesn't take a genius to attach silver studs, just a good, strong grip and some muscle."

"I think Louis and I can handle that." Ray beamed. "I'll go get them."

"Just a minute, Ray, and I'll go with you," Todd said. "You'll never get back into the camp unless I tell the guards it's okay."

Alex motioned Ray over as Todd ducked into the tent. "These friends of yours, Ray. Do I know them, too?"

"You know Robyn and Nicole better than I do. They're your other best friends. But they don't know anything about your powers, so be careful, okay?"

"That's not what I was worried about." Alex sighed. "They might be friends of mine, but I don't remember them. How am I going to explain that? I mean, what if they ask me a question I can't answer or something?"

"Man, I didn't think of that." Rubbing his chin, Ray stared at the ground. "Why not just tell them the truth? You've lost your memory."

"Because one of them may decide to go get the doctor even if we tell them not to." Alex frowned. "Why is that such a problem anyway? The idea of having a medical exam just makes my skin crawl."

"I'm not surprised," Ray said. "A doctor might

find out you've got this weird stuff in your system called GC-161—"

"Ready?" Todd dashed over, grinning from ear to ear. "I can't wait to see the look on Darian's face when I show up at the contest with my armor repaired."

Ray whispered to Alex as Todd started walking away. "Don't worry. I'll think of something."

"I sure hope so."

Todd looked back as Ray hurried to catch up. "You can let Thunder munch grass if you want, Alex. I'll put him away as soon as I get back."

Leading Thunder to a lush patch of grass, Alex watched until the boys were out of sight. She hoped they wouldn't be gone long. Todd had befriended her, a stranger in trouble, and she was grateful. But Ray was much more. She didn't remember him, but the close bond of friendship she felt was a welcome anchor in the vast sea of her forgotten life. Ray made her feel safe in the bizarre dream existence she had awakened to in the woods.

Alex's head spun as she considered her situation. Now that she knew Ray knew about her secret powers, they didn't seem quite so frightening. However, he had also made her realize that the danger she sensed from the unknown woman was real. Still, that didn't seem to pose any imminent threat.

At the moment, Alex was more anxious about meeting three other friends she didn't remember. She was sure she was going to make a complete jerk out of herself because she didn't have a clue about anything. Not them or school or even the project they were working on.

But she couldn't avoid them. Todd needed help fixing his gear, and Alex felt partially responsible for the damage. Without meaning to, she had gotten herself in the middle of the intense rivalry between the two candidates for knighthood. Her friendship with Todd might have made Darian mad enough to vandalize Todd's equipment.

"Lady Alex!"

"Hi, Lyric." Snapping out of her troubled thoughts, Alex waved at the elderly man hurrying toward her. Thunder raised his head and snorted as he chewed.

Huffing and puffing, Lyric paused a moment to catch his breath. "I'm so glad I found you."

"Is something wrong?" Alex asked, noting the minstrel's distressed expression.

"Yes." Clutching his lute, Lyric sighed. "Penrod's been telling people that you've got some fantastic magic power that could help Todd win the tournament."

Alex felt the blood drain from her face.

Her dangerous secret wasn't a secret anymore.

CHAPTER 11

Speechless, Alex just stared at Lyric for several seconds before she realized the old man didn't believe that she really had fantastic magic powers. He thought Penrod was just playing along with her pretend role of sorceress. The minstrel didn't know that she could be in major danger if the woman with the lab happened to hear the wild stories. Still, even though Lyric thought it was just a game, he was very upset.

"And Darian's going along with his little brother's story. You had every right to refuse to become his ally, Alex."

Alex sighed wearily. She still didn't remember

when Darian had asked her to form this alliance that had become the root of so much trouble.

The old man's eyes flashed with indignation. "So now, because you chose Todd and hurt his pride, Darian's smearing your name and accusing Todd of being a cheat."

"Accusing Todd!" Outraged, Alex reacted without thinking. "Darian's the one who snuck into Sir Ravenwood's tent and ruined Todd's armor." She stopped abruptly, covering her mouth with her hand.

"He did?" Lyric squared his narrow shoulders and spoke with calm resolve. "That is an unforgivable breach of honor, milady. Even worse than threatening a bard."

"I shouldn't have said anything, Lyric. Todd doesn't want anyone to know."

Puzzled, the elderly man frowned. "But such a grave misdeed cannot go unpunished."

"What can't?" Coming up on the far side of Thunder, Todd ducked under the horse's neck.

"Darian's deliberate destruction of your property," the minstrel said solemnly.

"I'm sorry, Todd," Alex said. "It just slipped out when Lyric said Darian was calling you a cheat."

Todd rolled his eyes and shrugged, as though

that didn't surprise or upset him. "I'll settle the score with Darian in the competition."

"There's more," Lyric said. "He's telling everyone that Lady Alex is a sorceress without honor."

"What?" Todd's demeanor changed from stoic acceptance to indignant fury in a split second. "That's not true!"

"We know that," Lyric said patiently, "but Alex is a stranger to the kingdoms. She doesn't have an established reputation and some people will believe Darian's lies."

"I don't want you worrying about my reputation," Alex interjected. "I just came here to work on a school project and got caught up in this SCA stuff accidently." *At least, that's what I think happened.* Her lost memory was really starting to be as annoying as it was unnerving.

"And I'm very glad you did." Smiling kindly, Lyric placed a protective hand on his lute. "And I don't want your first Renaissance Festival spoiled because Darian has an unfair personal grudge against you."

"He's right, Alex." Setting his jaw, Todd took Thunder's lead. "I'll defend your honor in the competition, too. And I'll win to prove your innocence."

Lyric shook his head in dismay. "In spite of the fun we have pretending to live by medieval rules, this is still the twentieth century. No one really thinks that truth and justice tip the scales in favor of whoever's right."

Todd's shoulders slumped as he nodded. "This is so unfair to Alex, though."

"Ah, but it's not hopeless." Lyric's face brightened and a mischievous twinkle lit up his eyes. "The truth has a way of coming out in the end."

"It does, doesn't it?" Todd nodded at the minstrel.

"Excuse me, milady." Lyric bowed as he took his leave. "I have a job to do."

Laughing, Todd pulled Thunder's head up from the grass. "Come on, Alex. We'd better get busy, too."

While Todd watered the horse and tied it back to the trailer, Alex wandered toward the tent, lost in thought. She felt terrible about the whole mess. Maybe she had insulted Darian and just didn't remember. One thing was certain, however. Although Darian and Todd had been rivals before, her presence had made the situation a lot worse.

Maybe, Alex thought despondently, *the best thing*

I can do for Todd and me is to ask Ray to take me home. Wherever that is! Ray had suggested that he could fill in the important blanks so she could muddle through until her memory returned.

Besides, if I'm gone, maybe Darian will lighten up on Todd. Except the damage was already done and Ray and her other forgotten friends were on their way to help fix it. If Todd didn't get his armor repaired, he wouldn't be allowed to enter the competition. Alex couldn't tolerate the idea of Darian becoming a knight by default.

"Hey, Alex!"

Ray shouted as he led a boy wearing a chain-mail headpiece, a dark-haired girl dressed in green, and a redheaded girl in a peasant blouse down the path between tents and trailers. They all looked vaguely familiar, too, but beyond that Alex was still completely blank. Todd came up beside her as Ray and his rescue team ran forward. Alex tried to relax, but her smile felt stiff and her knees shook as Ray's three companions began asking questions, all talking at once.

"Where did you get that gorgeous dress, Alex?" The redheaded girl raised her camera and snapped a picture of Alex and Todd.

"Uh—" Nervous, Alex hesitated. *Come on, Alex!*

That's an easy one! "Todd's uncle gave it to me after I fell in the creek."

"Well, no wonder you've been gone so long." The girl wearing green frowned. "What were you doing by the creek?"

"Getting water for Sir Ravenwood's horse."

"The guy who made the mounted joust finals?" The boy in chain mail whistled. "Cool!"

"If I had fallen in a creek, I would have had to spend the rest of the day wearing wet clothes." The redheaded girl sighed heavily.

"You look like a real girl, Alex," the other boy said bluntly.

Todd raised an eyebrow and grinned at Alex.

Alex shrugged.

"Sometimes you can be such a dork, Louis." The dark-haired girl eyed the short boy sternly, then smiled at Todd. "Hi. I'm Nicole."

"And this is Robyn." Ray glanced at Alex as he introduced everyone to Todd.

Alex fixed the names in her mind. *Louis, Nicole, and Robyn.*

"Don't you think we'd better get started on that gear?" Ray asked, taking control of the situation.

"We do if we want to finish on time," Todd said. "The tournament starts in just over an hour."

"Not a problem." Louis slipped his headpiece off and ran his hand through his sweat-dampened hair.

"Do you mind if I take pictures?" Robyn asked.

Todd shook his head. "Go ahead. We'll have to work out here because there's not enough room in the tent. Come on, Ray. You too, Louis."

"Uh—" Ray paused to look helplessly at Alex, then followed Todd to collect the armor and repair supplies.

"So what does a guy have to do to become a knight?" Louis asked as he disappeared through the canvas flaps.

"This is great, Alex," Robyn said as she shot a picture of the tent from an angle that included Sir Ravenwood's chair. "But why didn't you tell us you were planning to crash the inner circle? It was a brilliant idea."

"Well, uh—" *Wing it, Alex!* "I didn't exactly plan it. It just kind of happened."

"And how'd you manage to hook up with Todd?" Nicole sat down on a patch of grass. "He's great."

"I, uh—" Taking a deep breath, Alex calmed herself and sat down by Nicole. The girls didn't seem to suspect she didn't remember them, but as she did with Ray, she felt comfortable in their company. *Just don't panic . . . and tell the truth. Part of it anyway.* "He found me, actually."

Nicole leaned forward eagerly. "What happened?"

"I was in the woods—"

"The woods?" Robyn lowered the camera. "What were you doing in the woods? You were supposed to meet us by the acrobats right after the elephant ride, remember?"

No, I don't. Alex blinked and fought back a surge of sudden despair. *I don't remember!* In fact, she hadn't had any significant memory flashes since she had remembered being covered in icky gold stuff at the creek. Not even meeting her best friends had helped.

What if her memory *never* returned?

CHAPTER 12

Alex wrapped her arms around herself, chilled by the thought of never being able to remember her past or her family and friends. That would be almost as awful as being locked up by the frightening short-haired woman. Her life would still be lost to her—just in a different way.

And knowing that she had so many good friends would make the loss all the more tragic and painful.

"We were really worried, Alex," Nicole said. "We looked everywhere for you."

Robyn plopped down and set the camera aside. "When you didn't show up, I was absolutely sure something terrible had happened to you."

It did, Alex thought frantically. *I just don't know what it was.* She didn't blame them for being upset, but she didn't know how to explain.

"I want a persona, too," Louis announced as he came out of the tent with Todd's shield and scabbard.

"Maybe you can be Todd's squire after he becomes a knight," Ray suggested. He set down a box full of leather strips and thongs, tools, and silver studs.

"For the rest of the festival anyway," Todd agreed. *"If* I win the tournament."

"What are you talking about, Louis?" Nicole asked.

"I want to pretend to be a made-up character like Alex has been doing." Louis picked up a package of silver studs and watched attentively as Todd demonstrated how to use a metal punch to attach them to the leather.

"Like Alex?" Robyn and Nicole both looked at her.

"Yeah," Ray answered quickly. "She, uh—just kind of stumbled into the role-playing thing with Todd and, uh—grabbed the chance to really get into the festival."

"Why didn't you let us in on the fun, Alex?" Robyn faked a pout, then smiled.

"So who are you pretending to be?" Nicole asked.

"I don't know. I—" Alex answered Robyn first, then realized the answer fit both questions and faltered.

"Clever, huh?" Todd jumped in to cover Alex's truthful blunder. "When I met her, she pretended she was lost and couldn't remember her name. No self-respecting knight could abandon a lady in distress. So here we are."

Alex relaxed. Now if she couldn't answer a question or said something stupid, she had an excuse. She could blame it on her pretend memory loss.

Nicole gave Alex a thumbs-up and Todd an approving nod. "Good thinking, Alex!"

"The only thing that would have found me is poison ivy," Robyn muttered.

"It gets better." Sitting cross-legged on the ground, Louis went to work replacing missing studs on Todd's shield.

"Yeah." Ray nodded emphatically. "This Darian guy decided Alex is some kind of sorceress who insulted his family and is telling everyone she's a jerk."

Robyn blinked. "Now that sounds like something that would happen to *me.*"

"I'll say." Nicole's delighted grin became a furious frown. "Alex isn't a jerk, but this Darian character sure sounds like one. We've got to do something."

"I will." Todd turned his leather arm coverings upside down and began removing the stitching from the torn leather straps with a sharp, curved tool. "I'm going to defend her good name in the tournament."

"Trial by combat!" Louis's eyes gleamed with eager excitement. "Just like the old days. I can't wait."

Robyn and Nicole scowled at him.

Louis quickly qualified his remark. "It's all part of the game, guys!"

"Oh, yeah. Right." Robyn shrugged sheepishly.

It's a game to them, Alex thought as Todd threaded a large needle. *But not to me*. Because she had forgotten her old life, the medieval festival was the only reality she had right now.

Picking up an arm wrap and a new leather strap with stitch-holes already punched out, Todd glanced at Nicole. "Can you sew these together?"

"Sure." Nicole took the arm pad and positioned the holes in the leather strap over the holes in the armor.

"What about me?" Robyn asked.

"You can take the old straps off the leggings." Todd gave Robyn the stitch-ripping tool.

"Okay." Getting to work, Robyn bubbled over with enthusiasm. "You know, Alex. I was just telling Nicole how cool it was when knights used to defend a lady's honor in jousts and things. I never dreamed it would actually happen to one of us. You must be so thrilled!"

Alex just nodded. She wasn't thrilled at all. She didn't know why, but she wasn't comfortable having Todd settle her problem with Darian. It just didn't feel right.

"Is anyone hungry?" Louis asked.

"Yeah, come to think of it, I am." Todd glanced toward the far side of the field where the vendors and contestants parked their trucks. "There's a stand for participants over there. So we don't have to wait in long lines."

"I'll go." Anxious to have a few minutes alone to think, Alex jumped up. "You all seem to have everything else under control."

Taking everyone's orders and money, Alex lifted her skirt and hurried away. Oblivious to her surroundings, she stared at the ground as she walked. Why was she so bothered about Todd fighting for her in the tournament? In one way, it made her feel good to know Todd and her other friends wanted to help and defend her. Then she suddenly realized that if she didn't stand up to Darian herself, she would always be haunted by an ugly and crippling fear.

Because he wanted to avenge his insulted honor, Darian was using Penrod's story about her magic powers against her. She was afraid he might give her away to the short-haired woman who wanted to turn her into an experiment. So she had been hiding from him all day instead of meeting the problem head on and solving it.

Fear was her worst enemy.

Not Darian or the cold woman.

Alex didn't remember who she was, but she was suddenly sure of what she wasn't. She wasn't a coward. Giving in to fear meant forfeiting her freedom and self-respect, and she couldn't do that. Not even if she ended up spending the rest of her life in a stainless-steel lab.

"Hey! Magic lady!"

Snapping out of her deep thoughts, Alex looked back to see a young boy running toward her, waving a wooden sword. She was surprised to see that she had walked right by the food stand. A line of parked trucks stretched across the field several yards in front of her. A long row of tents and trailers facing the trucks formed a wide avenue in the field. Competitors sat in chairs preparing their gear and artisans worked on crafts to sell at their booths on the public side of the festival grounds.

"Where've you been?" Brandishing his small shield, the boy skidded to a halt. "I've been lookin' for you!"

"Why?" Alex asked curiously.

"Because." The boy heaved a long sigh. "It's my fault Darian doesn't like you."

As Alex stared at the boy's troubled face, another series of images flashed through her mind. The elephant ride, a wooded trail, and the small boy standing by a knight in silver armor. He was Darian's little brother, Penrod the Dragon Slayer.

"It's not your fault, Penrod."

"Yes, it is," Penrod insisted. "I told him you were mean to me on the elephant. And I shouldn't have lied, 'cause you were just making sure I didn't fall off and I know how mean and stubborn Darian can be. And I'm sorry."

"Thanks, Penrod. I appreciate that, but I don't blame you." Alex smiled, hoping to relieve the boy's guilt. She also hoped he might give her a clue about how to deal with his brother. "Why is he so mad at me, anyway?"

"He wanted to hang out with you and you said no." Penrod sighed again. "Sir Huxley's getting old and doesn't want to do the festivals anymore, and nobody else wants to be friends with him, either."

"Nobody? Why not?"

Penrod shrugged. "Maybe 'cause he's always trying to prove that he's better than everyone else."

Interesting, Alex thought. Except for when he was with Penrod, Darian had been alone every time she had seen him. Maybe Darian was his own worst enemy. He wanted friends, and yet he seemed to deliberately drive people away.

"Look out!" a frantic voice shouted. "Heads up!"

Penrod's eyes widened as he stared past Alex.

Hearing pounding hooves behind her, Alex turned.

A huge horse was barreling toward her and Penrod down the wide grassy lane between the trucks and tents.

A man wearing a blue denim shirt and blue jeans ran after the panicked runaway.

Another man washing out a cooler stumbled and

fell. Water jetted upward from the hose he held in his hand.

A woman spray-painting toy wooden shields dropped the paint can as she jumped out of the way. Gold paint sprayed out of the stuck nozzle.

Alex's eyes saw the horse, the hose, and the gold spray paint. In her mind, she saw a truck speeding toward her, then hitting a fire hydrant as she threw herself to the ground under a drenching rain of water and gold gunk.

Paralyzed by the barrage of shocking memories that suddenly came flooding back, Alex froze.

Directly in the path of the stampeding horse.

CHAPTER 13

"I'll save you!" Raising his toy sword, Penrod leaped in front of Alex.

Watching the thundering horse charge toward the boy instantly broke the stunned spell riveting Alex in place. She didn't have time to marvel at how instantly and completely her memory had been restored. She only had seconds to act before Penrod the Dragon Slayer was trampled.

"Hold, dragon!" Penrod yelled.

Simultaneously, Alex threw a protective force field around Penrod and telekinetically grabbed the broken lead rope dangling from the horse's halter. The animal's head snapped up in surprise as Alex jerked on the rope with all her mental might. It slowed, but continued forward.

"I said hold!" Clutching his shield and sword, Penrod took a step backward.

Alex yanked on the rope again. The powerful back legs slid under the horse as it planted its front feet and stopped.

"Wow!" Penrod looked back, his eyes shining. "How'd I do that?"

Since she couldn't tell the boy the truth, Alex decided to support his unexpected moment of glory. "You are Penrod the Dragon Slayer, aren't you?"

Penrod blinked, then grinned. "Yeah! I guess I am. I really am. Cool!"

"But you've reached your limit for this festival," Alex said sternly. She did not want to spend the rest of the day saving the boy from any more of his dangerous exploits. "Only one dragon per slayer, okay?"

Penrod glanced at the trembling horse as the breathless handler caught up to it and took the lead rope. The boy nodded slowly, as though he had just realized that luck had saved him from a severe injury. "Okay."

"Good." After assuring the horse's owner they were all right, Alex excused herself from Penrod and went to get her friends' snacks. While she waited for the order, she took a moment to enjoy the simple fact that she remembered everything about herself, her life, her friends, and family.

Alex grinned at the memory of the father-daughter golf tournament she had tried so hard to win before she found out her Dad really wanted to come in second so they wouldn't have to play again. Remembering the time she had messed up her mother's PR files because her mom had made her miss a new hit movie wasn't so pleasant. Mrs. Mack had almost lost the Paradise Valley Chemical account, but when the caterer cancelled out on Danielle Atron's fountain dedication, all Alex's friends had pitched in to help save her mom's job.

Alex was even glad she remembered Danielle Atron and the GC-161 accident that had given her the marvelous powers. And that the plant's chief executive officer desperately wanted to find the kid who had been exposed to the potent chemical. The danger of being discovered and locked in a lab was still there, but remembering relieved the immediate pressure. Besides, she and her brilliant older sister had become very close since the accident—and not just because Annie hoped to win a Nobel Prize for her research on Alex's amazing abilities and the illegal secret compound. Drawn together by Alex's need for help and Annie's scientific curiosity, they had gotten to know and respect each other.

A warm flush washed through Alex as she thought about her friends, especially Ray. She had met him years and years ago when he had almost run her down with his tricycle on the sidewalk in front of her house. They had been best friends ever since. Robyn's fatalistic view of the world and Nicole's determined efforts to save the world were qualities that distinguished them from the ordinary and Alex cherished their friendship. Even Louis, who could be charming and annoying at the same time, was a friend they could count on when things got tough. She had settled her differences with Louis after he first moved into Paradise Valley when he had stood up to the school bully to help Ray. They all accepted each other for the unique quirks that made them individuals and they were always there for each other when they were needed.

It's too bad Darian doesn't understand that, Alex reflected sadly.

"Sorceress!"

Alex stiffened at the sound of Darian's voice behind her, but she turned to regard him directly. She wasn't going to run away this time.

Darian's face was livid with rage. "What gives you the right to turn my brother against me?"

"I haven't done any such thing, Darian," Alex said calmly. "What makes you think I did?"

"Penrod's been down on me all day because he thinks I chased his magic lady away!"

"You did chase me away, Darian. You wouldn't listen when I tried to explain what happened on the elephant ride, because you were looking for a fight, not a friend."

Darian's temper flared. "I asked if you wanted to form an alliance and you said no."

"That's right." Alex's nerves and voice held steady in the face of Darian's intimidating demeanor. She was beginning to think his arrogant bravado might be a defense against rejection. Maybe he deliberately kept people from getting too close because he thought they'd leave him in the end anyway. It was also possible he didn't even know that's what he was doing. Now, he was afraid of losing his little brother, too—the only person who stuck by him—and Alex had to take advantage of that if she hoped to make a dent in his emotional armor. He might not take a hard-hitting hint, but it couldn't hurt to try.

"I didn't want to form an alliance with you or

anyone else, Darian. I came to the festival to learn about life in the Middle Ages for a school project."

"Oh, really!" Darian's dark eyes flashed. "Then why are you hanging around with Todd Chadwick? My worst enemy."

"Because," Alex answered honestly, "Todd and I are friends. You demanded an alliance. If you tried to be nice instead of pushing people around, you might find that some of us actually like you."

"Nobody likes me except Penrod, and now he's mad, too." Darian seemed almost sorry.

Alex took the cardboard tray from the woman behind the counter, weighing her next words carefully. "Maybe you haven't given anyone a chance, Darian. Friendship is kind of like all this SCA knight stuff you're into. You have to work at it and be honorable and honest and true." Shrugging apologetically, she turned to leave. "I'm sorry, but I've got to get back. My friends should almost be finished helping Todd with some last-minute equipment repairs."

Darian jerked back slightly, but he didn't say anything.

As Alex walked away, she felt Darian's gaze boring into her and wondered if she had done the right thing. Sometimes the truth hurt. But, she decided, even though it was hard, friends were straight with each other out of respect and concern. That's what made them real friends. She just hoped Darian understood that after he had a chance to think about it.

"What took you so long?" Setting down the stud-punch tool, Louis snatched a hot dog from the tray. "I'm famished."

"Me, too." Ray and Todd reached toward the tray together, then laughed.

Robyn and Nicole groaned.

Alex smiled. Everything was perfectly normal—exactly as she remembered it was supposed to be.

After wolfing down their hot dogs and drinks, the boys gathered Todd's repaired equipment. As they all headed for the arena entrance and the tournament, Alex felt her own excitement intensify. When she had suggested coming to the festival, she hadn't dreamed that they'd find themselves taking part in the actual events. That was thrilling.

While Louis helped Todd into his armor, Alex drew Ray aside. "I've got my memory back, Ray."

"Really? Great! What happened?"

"Well, I almost got run down by a horse. Guess the shock jolted my brain or something."

"Almost run down?" Ray's eyes narrowed. "You

didn't use your powers in front of anyone again, did you?"

Alex's eyes widened innocently. "No, not exactly. Actually, Penrod the Dragon Slayer saved me."

"So it's true?" Lyric walked up with his lute slung across his chest. "Penrod was just telling me all about it and I thought he was making it up."

"No, Lyric. It's true." Alex winked at Ray. She certainly couldn't tell the old man she had used her "magic" powers to stop the runaway horse. The minstrel would write a song about it and tell the whole world!

"Well, what do you know?" Lyric scratched his head, then shrugged. "I'm glad I found you anyway, Lady Alex. I've got something for you. Listen."

Alex recognized the tune Lyric played on his lute. It was called "Greensleeves," an old English folk song she had once tried to sing at an audition for a school talent show. But as she listened to the minstrel's mellow tenor voice, she realized he had changed the words.

By Squire Darian's spiteful lies,
Oh, Lady Alex, you have been wronged.

Defending your honor, the minstrel replies.
Let truth betrayed be avenged in song.

Ray grinned as he swayed to the melodic ballad, but Alex grew increasingly uncomfortable.

Disgrace and defeat shall be Darian's fame
For trying to ruin the good lady's name.

"Wait!" Alex hated to interrupt the old man, but she had no choice.

Lyric abruptly stopped singing. "What's the matter?"

"Uh—are you going to sing that song for everyone?" Alex asked cautiously.

"Of course!" Lyric glowed with pride. "Telling the truth about Darian is my way of paying you back for saving my lute. I just wanted you to hear it first."

"I think it's rad!" Ray said.

Alex sighed. "Well, if you're doing it as a favor to me, then as a favor to me, would you mind not singing it?"

Lyric looked puzzled, but not offended. "May I ask why not? It's true."

"I know, but Darian and I talked and we sort of worked things out." Alex struggled to explain without hurting the old man's feelings. "And, well—I think you did a great job on the song, but if Darian hears it, we'll never be friends."

"Friends?" Ray looked at her as if she were nuts.

"Well, not yet and maybe not ever, but everyone deserves a second chance, don't they?"

"Indeed, Lady Alex." Lyric nodded thoughtfully. "I will honor your wishes."

"Come on, you guys!" Louis called from the gate. "Todd's up next!"

"Thanks, Lyric." Alex waved as she and Ray ran to the staging area. Louis, Nicole, and Robyn stood near the arena, paying close attention as Sir Ravenwood explained how the competition was judged. Five other knights moved from squire to squire, carefully examining their equipment.

"The marshall is like a referee," the knight said, pointing to a man in full metal armor standing before the boys. "His word is law on the field."

Alex watched the inspection closely. The panel of knights did not seem impressed with Darian's armor and quickly moved on to the next boy. Darian glared at Todd when the knights nodded in appreciation of the time and craftsmanship that had gone into making his authentic-looking leather gear. Shaking her head, Alex sighed as the squires drew names from the marshall's helmet. Darian had no one but himself to blame if his armor didn't measure up.

"Lyric wouldn't go back on his word, would he, Alex?" Ray asked.

"I don't think so. Why?" Alex tensed as she looked up and saw Lyric wandering among the squires waiting by the gate. The old man was strumming his lute and singing, but he was too far away for Alex to hear.

The minstrel paused in front of Darian a moment. When the old man moved on, Darian followed him with a wide-eyed gaze. Alex couldn't believe Lyric would break his promise, but the look on Darian's face was one of total disbelief and shock. Turning slowly, Darian scanned the crowd until he spotted Alex and caught her eye.

Alex's high spirits were crushed in the intensity of Darian's unwavering stare.

She wasn't worried about herself any more.

Darian would get his revenge on Todd.

CHAPTER 14

Alex wasn't sure which made her feel worse: being betrayed by Lyric or causing more trouble between Todd and Darian.

The squires entered the arena and paused to bow before the king and queen sitting on their thrones in a raised, tented pavilion at the far end. Alex nodded at Todd as he strode back into the center of the field. As the boys paired off and the mock battle began, she alternated her attention between Todd and Darian.

"So let me get this straight." Louis leaned closer to Sir Ravenwood. "If the sword strikes the other guy's sword or shield, it's okay to hit hard, but they have to stop the force of the swing before they connect with body armor."

"Right." The tall, majestic knight looked down at Louis and smiled. "Control demonstrates skill. It's part of the art."

Nicole scowled. "I'm sorry, but I just can't see how whacking away at each other with bamboo sticks can possibly be considered an art form."

"It's a sport, Nicole," Ray said. "They even have fencing in the Olympics."

"Yeah," Louis said indignantly.

Alex held her breath as Todd's opponent swung hard. Todd raised his shield to take the blow, then swung his own wooden sword in a low arc. He pulled back slightly, barely tapping the other boy's thigh.

"Victory strike!" the marshall yelled.

"Does that mean Todd won?" Robyn asked.

"This round." Sir Ravenwood's face glowed with pride as Todd stood back, waiting for the others to finish the first match.

Minutes later, four defeated boys left the field. The marshall directed Todd to engage a taller boy wearing an elaborate cloth coat of arms over chain mail. Darian faced a sturdy boy dressed in the heavy metal armor of a later century than Robin Hood and King Richard the Lion-Hearted.

Alex almost hoped Darian would be defeated in this round so Todd wouldn't have to fight him, but that wasn't fair to Darian. In spite of his antagonistic attitude, inferior armor, and trash-can shield, his combat skills were finely honed. It wasn't long before the marshall declared Todd and Darian the winners of the second match.

"Way to go, Todd!" Nicole whistled and cheered as loud as everyone else.

Across the arena, Lyric slung his lute onto his back and positioned himself to view the final round. Watching him, Alex wondered if she had jumped to an unfair conclusion earlier. The minstrel was an honorable man. He wouldn't go back on his word. Maybe he had just stopped to warn Darian to fight fairly or maybe even to wish him good luck.

Ray edged up beside Sir Ravenwood. "If armor and sportsmanship count for fifty percent of the points, then doesn't Todd still have a chance to become a knight even if he doesn't beat Darian?"

"Theoretically, but the knights aren't bound by the point tally. They consider many different things before they vote and their decision is never questioned."

A roar went up from the crowd as the queen

dropped a flag to signal the start of the last, deciding match.

Alex's heart raced as the contest began.

Darian fended off Todd's blow with his shield and swung his wooden sword. Todd's sword swung up to connect with Darian's sword. *Whack!* The crowd shouted as sword struck sword in a series of lightning-fast clashes. Todd moved forward as he swung, pushing Darian back. Then Darian struck a staggering blow to Todd's shield that made him stumble.

"Oh, no!" Robyn's fingers dug into Alex's arm as Darian prepared to strike before Todd regained his footing.

Moving with agile grace, Todd ducked under Darian's bamboo blade. Surprised, Darian faltered and Todd touched his side with the end of his wooden sword.

"Victory strike!" The marshall raised his arms.

Todd hoisted his sword and shield over his head.

Darian froze.

"Now what am I going to do for a squire?" Sir Ravenwood looked exasperated for a second, then grinned.

As Todd turned his back on Darian to acknowledge the spectators, the cheer that started to rise from the crowd was suddenly silenced.

Darian drew back his sword to strike again.

"No, Darian," Alex whispered.

The marshall frowned and shouted, "Hold!"

"Don't do it, boy," Sir Ravenwood muttered.

"What's going on?" Louis asked, confused.

"The match has been called and Darian's made another threatening move," Sir Ravenwood explained. "That's not honorable. Todd has the right to forgive and forget it if he wants, but Darian will be totally disgraced and booted out of the SCA if he ignores the marshall's order to hold and strikes anyway."

Out of the corner of her eye, Alex saw Todd look back at Darian. Her focus was on the silver-coated knight with the wooden sword poised above his shoulder. Frozen in place, Darian met her gaze. Alex shook her head, silently pleading with him not to do something he'd always regret.

Everyone seemed to be holding their breath as Darian looked directly at Todd, bowed his head, lowered the sword, and then held it out in surrender.

Alex watched Todd watch Darian, then she heaved a huge sigh of relief as he grinned and clasped Darian's shoulder. Darian looked up uncertainly, then nodded.

"Hear ye! Hear ye!" A man ringing a bell entered the arena holding a scroll. "By unanimous decision, the noble knights of this festival declare that Todd Chadwick be granted the title of knight at the king's banquet tomorrow!"

Darian shook Todd's hand. Then both boys graciously bowed to the crowd and walked side by side toward the gate.

The cheer that followed was deafening.

Clutching her skirts, Alex ran with her friends toward the staging area. They all hung back as Sir Ravenwood pressed through the throng of contestants and SCA people surrounding Todd to offer their congratulations. After the knight gripped his nephew's raised hand and spoke into his ear, he joined the knights who had judged the competition.

When Todd spotted Alex and her friends waiting on the sidelines, he immediately excused himself and made his way through the celebrating mob.

"Thanks for helping me out, guys." Todd was still breathless after his exertion on the field. "I couldn't have done this without you. Especially you, Alex."

Alex fought to control a golden blush of embarrassment as she met Todd's gaze. "I wasn't much help, Todd. I think I caused you more trouble than anything else."

"No," Todd said with conviction. "You were an inspiration. Sir Ravenwood and I would be honored if you and your friends would be our guests at the king's banquet tomorrow night."

"Cool!" Louis whooped, then cocked his head. "Can we come back for the whole day and hang out with you, too?"

Todd nodded. "I'll have my uncle leave passes at the participants' gate."

"Thanks!" Grinning, Ray gave Todd an emphatic thumbs-up. "And congratulations on winning the tournament."

"I gotta admit, I was impressed," Nicole added.

"It's the most exciting thing I've ever seen!" Robyn exclaimed breathlessly.

Alex grinned, then saw Darian motioning to her from the fence. Curious, Alex excused herself and walked over. "What is it, Darian?"

Darian lowered his dark eyes as he shifted from one foot to the other. "I—uh, wanted to thank you. For saving me from Lyric's humiliating song."

"How did you know about that?" Alex asked, surprised.

"I told him," Lyric said.

Alex looked back.

The minstrel tipped his hat and smiled. "You acted like a friend, Alex, in spite of your differences with Darian. I thought he should know."

Alex beamed at the old minstrel. He hadn't broken his promise.

"I've been acting like a jerk and I'm sorry." Darian extended his hand.

"Don't worry about it." Alex shook his hand, then sighed as Darian nodded self-consciously and hurried off. Lyric went after him as Alex returned to her circle of friends.

"Well, I hope you're satisfied, Todd," Sir Ravenwood boomed as he joined the startled group. "Who's going to take care of my horse? Who's going to polish my armor and carry my lance now that you've become a knight?"

Everyone gaped at the towering man as he planted his feet, put his hands on his hips, and glared at his nephew. Sir Ravenwood looked as if he had just charged out of the pages of history.

Alex cleared her throat. "What about Darian? Sir Huxley's retiring, so he's a squire without a knight."

"Darian?" Ray blinked. "He doesn't deserve it after the way he's treated you and Todd."

"People change," Alex said. "And everyone deserves a second chance."

Louis scowled. "But won't Darian get kicked out of the SCA for raising his sword against Todd after the marshall called the match?"

Sir Ravenwood's pretend bluster faded as he glanced at his nephew. "Not if Todd forgives his indiscretion."

All heads turned to regard the new knight.

"Well." Frowning, Todd rubbed his chin. Then a slow smile spread across his face. "He's forgiven! My uncle's not going to let me off the hook just because I became a knight. Horses are a lot of work and I can use all the help I can get, if Darian's interested."

"Oh, I think he'll be interested," Alex said confidently. Not only was Sir Ravenwood one of the best mounted knights in the country, working with Todd and his uncle would help Darian restore his damaged honor.

"A good idea, Lady Alex. I'll give it serious consideration, but I need a squire *now!*" Sir Ravenwood roared. "The joust finals start in an hour."

"I'll do it," Louis offered.

"Excellent!" Waving his arm with a flourish, the knight strode off toward the royal reviewing stand. "Attend to my horse, Squire Louis!"

"Your horse?" Louis paled as he stared at the massive animal. "You mean *that* horse?"

"You can handle it." Grinning, Ray thumped Louis on the back.

"Relax, Louis," Todd said. "I'll take care of Thunder. No problem."

"Well, I've got a problem." Robyn rummaged through her drawstring bag, then started backing toward the main festival grounds. "I'm out of film. Don't you dare do anything cool until I get back, okay?"

"Okay!" Nicole hollered after her, then whispered to Alex, "With Robyn's luck, the guards won't let her back in the camp."

"If she's not back in half an hour, we'll go find her," Alex promised.

Alex, Nicole, and Ray began walking back to Sir Ravenwood's tent several yards behind Todd, who was leading the horse, and Louis, who had to jog to keep up. His chain-mail headpiece jingled and the wooden sword bounced against his leg.

Ray shook his head. "If our teacher was giving out A's for enthusiasm, Louis would cinch it for us."

"Better watch out, Ray," Nicole said with an amused gleam in her eye. "If you're not careful, wanna-be Sir Louis will be asking you to squire for him!"

Alex laughed. She would never forget the terrible loneliness and despair of not being able to remember anything. But in a way, losing her memory for a while had made her absolutely, one hundred percent certain of something very wonderful.

She loved her life.

Feeling a tug on her sleeve, Alex looked down to see Penrod looking up at her with a worried expression. "Hi, Penrod. What's the matter?"

"Nothing, I hope. I saw you talking to Darian by the fence. Is he bothering you again?" The boy frowned as he gripped the hilt of his wooden toy sword. " 'Cause if he is, I'll make him stop."

"No, Penrod, he wasn't bothering me. Actually, he apologized for being mean to me."

Penrod stopped dead and stared at Alex in openmouthed wonder.

"What?" Alex asked.

The boy gulped. "Nothing except a magic spell coulda made Darian do something nice! You really are a magic lady!"

Yeah, Alex thought with a mischievous wink, *I really am.*

About the Author

Diana G. Gallagher lives in Kansas with her husband, Marty Burke, two dogs, three cats, and a cranky parrot. When she's not writing, she likes to read and take long walks with the dogs.

A Hugo Award–winning illustrator, she is best known for her series *Woof: The House Dragon.* Her songs about humanity's future are sung throughout the world and have been recorded in cassette form: "Cosmic Concepts More Complete," "Star*Song," and "Fire Dream." Diana and Marty, an Irish folksinger, perform traditional and original music at science-fiction conventions.

Her first adult novel, *The Alien Dark,* appeared in 1990. She is also the author of a *Star Trek: Deep Space Nine*® novel for young readers, *Arcade,* and several other books in *The Secret World of Alex Mack* series, all available from Minstrel Books.

She is currently working on another *Star Trek* novel and a new *Alex Mack* story.